Special Agent Maximilian

SPECIAL AGENT MAXIMILIAN

Mimi Barbour

Sarna Publisher

Special Agent Maximilian

The Undercover FBI Series – Book 3

Contact Information: mimibarbour66@gmail.com

Cover Art by Steven Novak

Edited by Tessa Shapcott & Amanda Beaty

Proofread – Leandra Hanes

Praise for Mimi Barbour

Praise for the Undercover FBI Series

"As far as I know, I have read everything Mimi Barbour has published, and I bought most of them. I keep coming back because I love her sense of humor and style of writing and I always fall in love with her characters." ~ reviewed by A. Chambers

"Deserving of 10 stars! Love this series and highly recommend any and all books by Mimi! ~ reviewed by Shirleen Miller

"As a writer myself, I think that one of the true marks of an excellent author is solid, believable character development, and in my opinion, Mimi Barbour is the master of character development." ~reviewed by Flo Barnett

Dedication

I have one son. It's true – a fantastic child who I adore. And from the time he was born, there were two older boys in his life who he worshipped. He called them Mikki-Max, until he grew old enough to understand one was called Nik and the other's name was Max.

Every week for many years, these two brothers joined us for Sunday dinner along with their wonderful, funny, endearing father. As I watched them grow up, they taught me so many things – mainly how not to be too overprotective and to give my kid breathing space to be independent. For those lessons, I'm so grateful.

Today, I'm incredibly proud of these two men and their accomplishments. And so I wrote Special Agent Maximilian and am now dedicating this book to them….for Mikki/Max!

Love you guys!

Undercover FBI Series
— Popular & Compelling! —
Special Agent Francesca (Book 1)
Special Agent Finnegan (Book 2)
Special Agent Maximilian (Book 3)
Special Agent Kandice (Book 4 – to be released Winter 2015)

***

Holiday Heartwarmers Trilogy
— Truly a Christmas favorite! —
Please Keep Me (to be released Oct 2015 Book 1)
Snow Pup (to be released Nov 2015 Book 2)
Find Me a Home (to be released Nov 2015 Book 3)
Holiday Heartwarmers Trilogy Box Set (to be released Dec 2015)

***

Other Titles
I'm No Angel
Hotshot Cowboy
Big Girls Don't Cry
Christmas Runaway
The Surrogate's Secret
Mimi's Mix (Box Set)
'Tis the Season (Box Set)
Hearts, Flowers & Romance (Box Set)
Dangerous Encounters (Multi-author Box Set)
Ten Christmas Brides (Box Set with 9 other authors)

***

All Mimi's books can be found on her Amazon Author Page:
http://bit.ly/MimiBarbourAmazon OR
Website: http://mimibarbour.com

Chapter 1

From the corner of his eye, Nik saw the redhead approaching, hair flying, face full of anger. He managed to duck in time to elude the fist aimed at his face, but the one that plowed into his belly caught him off guard.

"Maximilian Foster! Where the *hell* have you been? I've searched high and low for your sorry ass for more'n a month. Everyone thinks you're dead. And where do I find you? Sauntering in the French market as if you haven't a care in the world."

Imprisoning her wrists before she did major damage seemed to be the most intelligent thing for Nik to do, but he hadn't realized her skill. In seconds, she had him pinned to the wall of the shop next to where he stood—not wanting to hurt her, he'd let it happen.

"Lady, what the hell is wrong with you?" He stamped down on his rising frustration. *What's going on with this crazy dame?*

"What's wrong with me? *What's wrong with... are you kidding me?* We're partners, or have you forgotten that insignificant detail, and that it used to mean something?"

Ah! So this was Max's partner, Maya Barnes. Now what the hell was he going to do? Recently, he'd made the decision to fake being his twin, pretend he was Max Foster. But maybe he'd gone and spoiled the chance. Thinking quickly, he attempted to recover lost ground.

"Maya? I'm sorry... I–I don't remember. I don't remember anything. I've been wandering around here praying something would be familiar. I'm sorry, I..." He choked on the word *sorry* since it wasn't a word he was familiar with, but he knew his brother used it a lot. That stupid word, along with his twin's winning smile, had no doubt gotten Max out of a lot of scrapes.

"Dammit, Max, don't try using that idiotic grin on me. You know it doesn't work. We've been hunting for you for weeks. One day you were there and the next you'd disappeared. I figured the Mosleys had gotten you once you'd let it out that we were on to them."

Mosleys? She had it half right. They had been after Max, and in the end had put a hit on him. Only they weren't a local gang as the department thought. It went a lot deeper than just New Orleans bad boys. Seemingly, Max had clued into their operation, which had led back to Los Angeles. And it hadn't only been drugs. Nope! Things had gone deeper and dirtier than even he'd suspected.

Nik pretended a weakness he didn't feel and let his body slouch to the side. At first her green sparklers flared with suspicion, then softness flooded her expression and she supported rather than shoved.

"Oh God, Max. I'm sorry. You really are in a bad way, aren't you? Come on, let me help you. We'll grab a cup of coffee and you can tell me what happened."

Playing this lady while she was pissed hadn't bothered Nik whatsoever, but lying to her when those big eyes plied him with an affectionate pity was another thing altogether. What the hell was he to do now?

"I don't really want coffee, Maya. Maybe I could just come to the office."

Not taking his refusal seriously, Maya wrapped her arm around his body, clamped her fingers on his wrist and half dragged him through the open doors to a nearby table at Café du Monde. She led him to a seat and sat across from him. "Don't be silly, you love coffee. Look, you're a rotten son-of-a-bitch, but I'm glad to see you. I couldn't believe you'd leave me high and dry, worrying myself sick about what could have happened. Now it all makes sense."

Shaking his head, not understanding her logic, he just stared at her and waited. No doubt she'd enlighten him as to what she meant. He must have shown his lack of understanding because she assumed a disgusted look. "Stop being so dense! You might be a philandering S.O.B. and an unmitigated snob, but I'd never have believed you would treat me so shabbily. I guess I'm relieved to see I was right."

"You're relieved to know I can't remember anything? That I woke up in the ditch with a lump the size of an extra-large egg on the back of my head? God save me from trying to analyze the labyrinth of a female's mind."

Maya sat with her mouth open; her eyes focused and didn't utter a word. With a laser-like gaze, she drilled every spot of his face and then shook her head. "Even dressed like an army store reject, I'd swear you were Special Agent Maximilian Foster. Then you say something and I have to admit to having huge doubts. And just so you know, Max'd die before appearing in public looking like G.I. Joe."

Nik had seconds to decide his future. To make up his mind if he was serious about going after the people who'd beaten his brother and left him broken, covered in blood and lying in a ditch. Guessing there had never really been a choice, he replied softly, "I'm sorry, Maya. You're the first person I've remembered, even remotely. That is, I know your name, but that's about it. You have to believe me when I tell you that I can't remember anything after being struck. My own clothes were covered in blood and I got these cheap. After all, I only had ten bucks in my pocket—no wallet, no I.D. I'm a mess, and I guess I need your help." Instinctively, watching the caring flood her face, he reached out his hand and she grasped his fingers and squeezed. Hard.

Her eyes, piercing green shards, speared him. "You lying piece of shit. I don't know what your game is but you aren't, and never could be, Max. Now who the hell are you and what's going on?"

Chapter 2

Maya had no doubt at all that the man sitting across from her was not her partner. He didn't have that same sly grin, or the habit of letting his gaze slide away when the subject got uncomfortable. This one looked her straight in the eye and never smiled at all.

Before she could follow up her confrontation, his narrow-eyed stare transferred to something happening behind her. A nasty male voice shouting about sloppy brats registered, next a fist hit the table, the sound loud and threatening. Then a woman's voice pleading, "Sandi didn't mean to spill it, Hank," sunk in.

To her utter shock, Max, or whoever he was, flew from a sitting position to lunge across the room. His speed stunned her. When motivation demanded any excess energy, Maya knew her Max could move fast, but this guy was supersonic. One minute, he sat facing her and the next he was gripping the raised arm of a man two tables away.

Not being any slouch herself, she quickly followed and saw what was going down. Max's double had a fat dude in a hold that denied him any leverage to fight back, while a little girl, no more than five years old, with spilled juice dripping from the front of her dress and down the table, became hysterical. The woman, who Maya presumed to be the child's mother, looked frozen from fear.

Taking in the situation as she was trained to do, Maya crouched down so she could gather the little one close and calm her. Watching the struggle taking place between the two men, she motioned to the frozen woman to come to her and get away from the action that could erupt at any minute. Mind you, Max's double seemed to be in complete control of the situation. Looking bored by the bullying antics the slimeball was trying to pull, he tightened his hold. Doing something amazing with the fingers of his right hand near the other man's neck, she watched as the big bruiser slumped into unconsciousness.

Max's double lowered the guy's body onto a chair, leaning him against a pillar and positioning him to look as if he was napping. Then he picked up the other fallen chair before he turned toward the shaking woman still frozen in place, unable to move. He took her arm and guided her away from the rest of the crowd. With his head bent to listen, it was obvious that his gentle manner soothed her.

Maya couldn't hear what was being said, but she saw him take a wad of money from his pocket, hold it out to the crying mom and wrap her fingers around it so she clutched it tightly.

She switched her attention to the sobbing child in her arms. "I hate Hank. He's a big ol' meanie." Though the words were whispered, Maya heard them loud and clear.

"Is he your daddy?" Knowing that nowadays nothing could be taken for granted, she decided to get the information rather than chastising the girl.

"No! And I wished he didn't live with us. He's a big poopy-mouth, so there." Sniffling, her face once again hidden in Maya's neck, the almost-baby clung tight and began to wail loudly.

Hiding her grin, Maya rocked back and forth, trying to calm the child as best she could until the mother's reaching hands came into view. Maya transferred the shaking little person into the arms of the still terrified, embarrassed woman. With eyes full of tears and something else that looked like hope, the mother hugged her darling close. Maya questioned, "Are you okay?"

Skinny and trembling, her blonde hair scraped back into a pony-tail that did her no justice, the mom smiled shakily and nodded. "I am now. Your man just gave me the means to escape, and Sandi and I will be free. We'll go and gather our things from the trailer and be on the next bus before Hank can find us." After she had spoken, she opened her fist to show a stack of bills that looked to be at least five hundred dollars.

Maya patted her shoulder and smiled. "I'll hang here until the cops come and arrest Hank for disturbing the peace. By the time they get him to the station and take their time booking him, it should give you a few more hours to make your escape."

"Bless you. That'll really help. I'll be able to properly quit my job and get the money owed before we leave." The tears flowed steadily now. "I've been trapped for what seems like forever. I can't believe we'll soon be free."

"We going to leave Hank, Mama?" Wet eyes glowing, the little doll patted her mother's cheek to get her attention.

"Yes, baby. We're going on a bus trip, just you and me."

"Goody!"

Amazed how quickly a youngster's tears could end when happiness flooded out fear, Maya shared their pleasure with a spontaneous hug that made the world brighter. Then, she kissed the baby cheek of the now excited and happy little angel. Looking at the mom, she added. "Good luck, honey. You get away from that idiot and find a nice place to settle down. Make sure it's safe, and introduce yourself to the local police; let them know about this scum, and that you want a restraining order placed in case he finds you."

Waving to Sandi as the two rushed away, Maya checked the sleeping fool to be sure he was still out cold and pulled her phone from her pocket. She scanned the restaurant for Max's double. Last time she'd seen him, he'd been talking to the owner and soothing ruffled feathers. Now he was nowhere to be found.

"Aw, shit! Not again."

Chapter 3

Nik knew he shouldn't have disappeared from the restaurant and left Maya to deal with everything, but he needed time to think. After all, before his capture, his twin brother Max had come to him for help and he'd promised to do whatever he could.

Unfortunately, the incident in the cafe had put the fear of God into Nik. He'd used every ounce of willpower he could dredge up not to damage that child-abusing bastard in a really bad way. Mind churning with fury, his hands had itched to leave lasting scars. Hearing the brutal manner the asshole had used with the little one had brought back memories best forgotten. Memories he couldn't seem to push back into the niche in his head where they'd been stored for years.

As he walked, the military counselor's warnings popped into his head. He'd been forced to retreat from active duty for the time being because of an injury and insomnia—most likely caused by a form of PTSD. Thinking back at how he, and a lot of his friends, had scoffed at the idea of Post Traumatic Stress Disorder, thinking themselves immune, he shook his head at their insensitive stupidity.

What had the doc said? No anxieties or hassles! No alcohol and absolutely no drugs. Exercise, good food, lots of sleep; then the nightmares would fade and the panic would be more controllable.

Since he drank very little and never did drugs, or hadn't since his misspent youth, that hadn't been a problem for him. As far as the stress went—well, that seemed to be his biggest threat.

On the other hand, earlier, when he reacted to the circumstances at the restaurant, he hadn't lost control. Tough as it had been, he'd stayed cool. Though his heart had taken a shit-kicking, much more than it used to when he'd been in dire situations, it hadn't choked him or made him lose consciousness. Not like the last time.

Christ, if only he could beat this PTSD crap and get on with his life. Since he'd been on leave and left the Navy Seals in Iraq four months ago, he'd drifted, never feeling at peace, never knowing who he was and what he wanted. Traveling had seemed to be the answer. He'd started on the East coast, heading west until he'd stopped in New Orleans, a city that had grabbed hold and, for some strange reason, couldn't be shaken loose.

Then he'd run into his twin brother.

What a hell of a shocker that was. Imagine being in a Starbucks, and having the replica of yourself ask if you were in line or just checking the menu. The disbelief still rippled through his body at the memory. Both men had been stunned.

"Holy shit, you look like me." Max had started the conversation.

"Nope! You mean—you look like me." Nik couldn't

resist the jibe and stiffened when he saw his lookalike's sly grin and nod. He'd seen that same expression many times from his old man, usually before his fist flew.

"Have it your way, bro. But the resemblance is so strong, we could be twins."

Interrupted by the barista, they each ordered the same drink—the Red Eye—and moved to the side to pick them up. While waiting, both examined the other until Max spoke. "It's creepy in a way, seeing your double. I mean I've heard of this sort of thing happening, but I never thought it would to me."

Nik took in Max's FBI badge and his fancy duds and two seconds later he'd made up his mind. "Do you have a few minutes? I think we need to talk."

Max's eyebrows rose at the tone and his grin slipped. Then he shrugged. "Yeah! Sure. Wanna stay here?"

"It's as good a place as any." Nik picked up the first cup and handed it to Max, and then retrieved his own. He led them to a seat at the back of the restaurant.

Once Max had removed his suit jacket and placed it, folded neatly, on the empty chair, he pulled up his sleek pants, to accommodate him sitting, and leaned back confidently. "So... what's your name?"

"Nik Baudin. Yours?"

"Max Baudin Foster."

"Holy shit!" Shock washed over Nik, leaving him weak-kneed and dumbfounded. His ol' man had mumbled through his drunken fits about another son, but Nik had put it down to the ramblings of an intoxicated idiot. After seeing Max at the counter and gauging how alike they were, he'd just had to know for sure. Now he did. The rioting going on inside his stomach didn't bode well for him getting much sleep that night.

Max's features had solidified, and Nik watched as a myriad of emotions fought for control. "Holy shit is right! We must be brothers." He pulled out his phone and pushing one button, he arrogantly held up his finger to stop Nik from talking and waited.

Since Nik had nothing to say, he took a gulp from his favorite coffee instead and felt as if he'd choke. Pushing the cup away, a sour thought attacked. *Dammit, I'd been looking forward to that drink!*

Surreptitiously, leaning over the table with his elbows on the chair arms, he intertwined his fingers using them to ram his stomach where vicious stabs of fire attacked. The forgotten lower back cramps returned with a vengeance. Using the techniques he'd learned from an old girlfriend who was a yoga instructor, he stretched slowly, inconspicuously, and exhaled; forcing his stomach muscles in, and then took a huge breath, filling his lungs. A few of these miraculous movements and peace returned to the irritated region. At least he didn't feel as if his next move would be with his head in a toilet.

Without being able to stop himself, he explored the features of his lookalike and thought that it was rather a miracle. True, his brother's shorter hair was slicked up in a style that the suits wore today, with the front shoved ridiculously high, as if any normal guy would want to look like he'd had a shock and his hair had gotten the worst of it. Pathetic! On the other hand, Max's suit looked as if it had been made just for him: silky gray, slick, in a modern fashion, and fitting perfectly.

What got Nik the most was the blue tie Max was viciously loosening that matched the exact color of his eyes. For the first time Nik understood why women went so goofy over his own. They were mesmerizing; the depth of the blue surrounded by the black limbal ring around the iris drew you in and made it almost impossible to look away.

Max's voice broke into his thoughts and one word blew his mind.

"Mom? We need to talk. Are you at home? I have some-one here you should meet." Max's face hardened. "You don't need your hair done. You keep putting that all that spray on and it'll start falling out and you'll go bald. I'll be there shortly. And get prepared for a shock." Max hung up the phone and stared at Nik. "You coming?" As if he were used to being in charge, he stood and grabbed his suit jacket viciously. Then he walked out as if he had no doubt whatsoever that his new-found brother would obey.

Mom?

Stunned by being treated so callously, so unlike the way he'd ever allowed anyone to treat him, Nik stood and followed. How could he not? *Mom!* For the first time in his life, he was going to meet his mother. The woman about whom his father had told him lies. "The bitch is dead and good riddance," covered it about right.

Chapter 4

Following Max to his silver Lexus CT, a showy vehicle which didn't surprise Nik whatsoever, he got into the passenger seat and sat quietly, waiting for his brother to start a conversation.

"You're a quiet one, aren't you?"

"Could say the same for you. We've been driving ten minutes and you haven't said a word."

"I've been thinking about all the lies Mom has told me over the years. When I was a little boy, I wanted a brother because all the other kids had them. She said she couldn't give me any brothers, and that there would always just be the two of us. It made her sad so I stopped asking."

"Did she ever remarry? I know her and the old man *were* married because I found a wedding picture. When I showed it to him, he ripped it up and said that she'd died." Nik didn't use the exact words that had been used, but he remembered how they'd made him feel. *Hopeless!*

Max's head swiveled to Nik. "Hell, why would he lie to you and tear up a photo of her?"

Nik angled his head sideways and stared at Max.

"You're asking me about him? Hell, bro, they *both* lied. I guess she left him and I can't say I blame her. He was a mean son-of-a-bitch."

"Was?"

"Yeah. He was killed in a bar fight while I was on my last deployment. The way the boozer carried on, I'm surprised he lasted as long as he did. I'd escaped the asshole at sixteen and hoped never to hear from him again. As his next of kin, they contacted me when I was overseas to inform me of his death, and about where to pick up his remains. Far as I'm concerned, they can keep him."

"I'd like to have known him. I always wanted to have a dad."

"No. You wouldn't. He wasn't a dad. He was a mean prick who liked nothing better than to see people squirm."

"Still, she left him and I never got to meet him at all."

Christ, man, you don't know how lucky you were. Before he could stop the words from escaping, Nik admitted, "You know it sounds weird, but there was always something missing. I'd find myself looking around at everyone.... Shit! I don't know what the hell I'm talking about."

Max was listening. His head was cocked toward Nik in a familiar way that Nik recognized. He did the same thing himself when he concentrated on another person. But it seemed strange to see his lookalike using the identical mannerism.

"I know what you mean. As a young boy, I had dreams that there were two of me. I'd wake up crying and when I finally told my mom about them, she had a nervous breakdown. Cried for days. Scared the hell out of me. I never mentioned them again. They lasted until I started high school, and then they stopped."

Max pulled into the driveway of a lovely historic-styled

home in the French Quarter that screwed with the tempo of Nik's heart. He recognized the place. *This is the house in my dreams.* It was a magnificent Victorian on Esplanade Avenue, with fancy arches and a black wrought-iron balcony running across the front on the upper floor. Baskets of flowering plants were scattered everywhere and added a nice touch.

To Nik, it looked like a palace. Compared to the dumps he'd lived in as a boy, it was paradise. "This is where your mom... our mom lives?"

"She inherited it from the aunt we moved in with. The old battle-axe let us live with her as long as Mom nursed her. Aunt Vi was a widow and had cancer. This house belonged to Vi's husband's family, but they've died out now. The only people she could leave it to were Mom and me. It probably killed her to do so—the old witch was a cheapskate—but she loved the house too much to see it go into a stranger's hands. Thank God."

Max got out of the car and started toward the back of the house, taking for granted that Nik would follow. He did, his eyes spellbound by the splendor of a house that he'd fallen in love with the first time he'd dreamed about it. As a boy, the only joy he'd ever felt was at night while fast asleep, dreaming of this house. It had been vague, true. But he'd recognized it instantly.

Inside, Max led him down a hallway full of antiques, the hardwood gleaming, and into a small sitting room. There sat a woman waiting, her back toward them. When she heard them enter, she turned and screamed.

Then she fainted.

Chapter 5

"Christ, it's just like her to pull a stunt like this." Furious, Max moved forward to haul his mother up off the floor. Before he could start to lift her, Nik's arms had scooped her close and he gently lowered her to the sofa. He unbuttoned her tight collar. "Get some water for her; she'll want some when she comes to."

Max hesitated, anger still coloring his expression, but he did as Nik ordered.

Within a few minutes, the woman's eyelids fluttered and her trembling hand reached toward her throat. Nik took the water from Max. "What's her name?"

"Mom."

"Don't be a smartass." Nik couldn't believe that Max would make jokes at a time like this. Their mother lay on the couch, having had the shock of her life, and Max seemed to think it was amusing.

"Look, her name is Nellie and she pulls these faints whenever she has to deal with a crisis. It's her way. She always comes out of them in the end. When I was a boy, they used to terrify me. Now—not so much."

The faint moan caught both men's attentions. What finished them was the wail of pain that followed. It made the hairs on the back of Nik's head stand straight up, and he felt his skin pebble up his arms and around his back. Shivers attacked, leaving him extremely uncomfortable. He'd rather face a platoon of snipers than this one tiny woman.

"Max?"

"I'm here, Mom."

"Who's with you?" Nellie's eyes were scrunched closed. It was almost comical.

"My brother, Nik Baudin."

"I thought you were going to say that. Is he still here?"

"Yes, Mom. He's holding your hand."

With her eyes closed, Nellie moved her other hand over Nik's and grasped tightly. "My Nik. My own baby boy. I never dreamed this day would come. Or that you were alive."

Nik swallowed the lump that was choking him. "The Bastard told me you were dead. I never knew I was a twin, or that you were alive. If I had known, I would have come to find you."

Her eyes opened slowly. She stared at him, searching each feature. He returned her gaze, getting lost in the blue depths of her still gorgeous eyes. Sparkling from tears, they glowed, the light of love blazing at him so strongly it stunned him, weakened him—made him sob inside, which scared him.

She blinked away the unremitting tears. "The Bastard told you I'd died? I don't understand."

Hatred for the man who had been his father curdled Nik's emotions. Before he could speak, he had to swallow the bile that churned and threatened to erupt.

Stunned, he repeated himself. "I never knew you were alive, or that I had a brother."

Nellie sat up and slumped back against the cushions, careful not to let go of Nik's hand. She looked over at Max. But he said nothing. So she swiped at her nose with the wad of tissues Max had handed her and began to talk.

"I like your name for him, used it over the years myself a time or two. Hang on, Max. I'm getting to it."

Nellie waved Max away after he'd made an impatient move towards her. Then she turned back to Nik, her eyes begging for forgiveness. "In a nutshell, the *Bastard* beat me until I hated the sight of him. One night, Nik, you woke up. Even as a two-year-old, you ran up to him and yelled for him to stop. And so he turned on you. He hit you hard. You flew against the wall and lost consciousness. I was in no condition to go with you to the hospital, so he took you himself. I guess it scared him. He'd hurt you too badly to ignore your injuries.

While he was gone, I called my brother-in-law. He and my sister were in town and had invited us to visit with them at their hotel. It was the reason your father had lost his temper in the first place. He'd refused to let me see them, and, for once in my life, I'd argued. 'No way,' he'd screamed. I'd never seen him so furious. But it had been years and I really wanted to visit with her. Of course, he'd made sure it wouldn't happen. Or thought he had."

"Once he'd left with you, I called a taxi, packed up Max and left, went to my sister's hotel and they took me in. I called him the next day to tell him I was leaving him and taking you boys with me, and he was livid. 'Don't bother going to the hospital,' he'd said. That's when he told me you had died and if I wanted to leave, fine. To get the hell out of his life and not to come crawling back or he'd take

Max and kill me. God forgive me, I believed the Bastard."

Max interrupted. "You mean you never checked with the hospital, Mom? How could you be so dense?"

"Hey? Back off, bro. Let her finish." Nik surged to his feet, and Max's blink of surprise halted his forward momentum, stopped him from beating the crap out of his newly found, short-tempered brother. His glare worked and Max shrugged and stayed where he was. Nik resumed his seat beside Nellie and patted her hand. "Go on."

"Of course I did, Max. But I wasn't in any shape to go to the hospital myself. Your father had thrashed me worse than usual and had broken two of my ribs. Besides, I'd collapsed from hearing the horrible news about Nikky, so my brother-in-law made the trip instead. When he returned to the hotel, he confirmed that you had died and your father had already made arrangements with the hospital. I was in agony, broken-hearted, and couldn't seem to snap out of it. I found out later that Vi had drugged me to calm me down and the pills had had an adverse effect on me. I was a zombie. So, my sister and brother-in-law packed me and Max up and brought us to their home here in New Orleans." Exhausted by her speech, Nellie started to sob.

Max finally came close and rubbed her shoulders. "Uncle Ed was a real bastard, too, Nik. Chances are, he made a deal with our father to keep quiet about your recovery. To an asshole like him, it would have seemed fair for them each to keep a child. Besides, he knew that Mom would never have come here to look after them if she'd known you were still alive. Both my aunt and uncle used Mom as their personal maid and nurse until the day he passed on, then she followed a few years ago."

Nik shook his head, disbelieving the cruelty of some people. It never ceased to amaze him how folks could treat others so inhumanely.

In a voice softened from caring, he murmured, "I'm so sorry, Nellie. That this had to happen to you." Caressing her hand, he squeezed it gently.

Nellie's head shot up and she yanked her fingers from his to point at him. "This didn't just happen to me, Nik Baudin. It happened to us. And my name is Mom."

Chapter 6

Maya couldn't believe that Max, or whoever it was she'd run into today, could do this to her again. That son-of-a-bitch drove her crazy. Her partner's whims were the bane of her existence and if he wasn't such a good agent, she'd have asked for a transfer a long time ago. Fisting her hands, nails digging into soft skin, she huffed out a breath and relaxed. Who was she trying to kid?

New Orleans had been home for her ever since she'd come with her family years ago and it would be hard to pull up roots now. Something about the place had grabbed her heartstrings and wouldn't let go. Whether it was the spicy seafood treats and fried oyster po'boys, the diversity and eccentricities of this port city, or the feeling of history that could be seen if one cared to look, she didn't know. All she knew was when it had come time for her to fill out the box on the FBI's form for where she'd prefer to be posted; she'd filled in New Orleans.

Not once had she regretted her decision. She lived far enough away from her needy family that she could go back periodically and not expect too many return visits, thank goodness. Between her mother and two sisters, there might be enough brain power to rule one simpleton. Those women didn't have a clue. Men and money, in that order, were all they cared about.

Her mom was a single mother who'd had three girls to raise; she'd done so by attaching herself to the first willing man, rather than working at a career in order to provide. Maya and her sisters had grown up with so many step-dads that she couldn't remember their names anymore. Some had been nice while others had been assholes, most had been cheap, and all were gone.

Sadly, the one who Maya had considered her only true father had died young. A black man with a pure-gold heart and a talent for the clarinet, Sam Brown had been the one who'd made sure she didn't become like the others. He'd spent enough time with the idealistic young girl to explain the intricacies of life, the importance of self-respect and personal values.

In her early teens, the dreamer years where optimism and impracticality ruled, he'd made a huge impact. Life had been good when they'd lived with Sam. He'd adored her mother and treated her like a lady, same with her daughters. That lesson had become ingrained in Maya. She knew she couldn't settle for less and still hadn't found a guy with Sam's special gifts.

Sheila and Kerrie, Maya's two sisters, hadn't been as affected by Sam's charms. When he'd been around they'd been older, at the budding stage—that border between teenage silliness and an *I'm a woman now* mentality.

They were both man crazy. Power over the male species meant wiggling their gorgeous tushes and submitting their lush bodies for the attentions they seemed to crave. Not a problem whatsoever, as long as it got them what they wanted: a good time and a man to rule their world.

Not so for Maya. Never!

During the years they'd lived with him, Sam had accepted a gig in New Orleans with his band at Preservation Hall, and had brought the family to a small, quaint house he owned near the Mississippi. They'd had a wonderful year before leaving to go back to Los Angelas.

Throughout those months, her love for the city had solidified. They'd spent every hour he'd had free touring the places where he'd hung out as a boy, touristy spots like Bourbon Street and the famous French Quarter. They'd even fished on the bayou and taken multiple riverboat cruises. On those wonderful days, he'd cemented her love for the local food and music. Sneaking her into the Hall to hear him play his jazz had delighted her, and it had cultivated an undying love for those incredible sounds.

One day in particular haunted her often. He'd taken her on yet another riverboat cruise and they'd sat outside in the shaded deck area talking as usual.

"Don't be so hard on your sisters. They can't help being the people they are. No one taught them any different."

"Like you're teaching me?" Maya had reached for his hand and after he'd gently wrapped his long artist's fingers around her smaller ones, she'd hung on.

"You could say that. But, sugar-baby, you're a sponge. I never knew anyone who wanted so bad to learn everything she could."

"Because I'm not like them, I don't get how they think. All they care about is boyfriends, clothes, and hairdos. What does that matter? What about the poor and homeless? What about the crime rate and the lack of federal help here in New Orleans? What about—"

"Maya, not everyone arrives in this crazy ol' world with a civil conscience. Most don't. Maybe they'll learn to care as they grow older. But you're one of those rare people who were born giving a damn. You never want to lose that, sweetheart. It's what makes you stand out from the sleepers, makes you special. You know what I mean?"

"Like the way you feel when you're playing your music?"

"That's right. I'm one with God when my clarinet is singing sweetly and I'm entertaining the folks. No better feeling in the world than doing what you were meant to do."

"Sam, what do you think I was meant to do?"

"Shoot, child. From the way you're always trying to look after your family, I'd say you need to be in law enforcement."

Maya had giggled while he'd roared. The private joke was shared between them and had given her one of her favorite memories of their times together. They'd laughed because lately her sisters had started using the phrase, "What are you, a cop?" so often that even her mother had spit it at her. All she'd done was question them about their antics and habit of disappearing without notice.

Visiting the past, Maya was so deep in her thoughts that she wasn't aware of the approaching officers until one spoke.

"Ma'am, is this sleeping beauty here the perp?"

Coming back to the present with a start, Maya nodded at the two uniforms who were standing in front of the table where old Hank, groggy and garbling, was beginning to regain consciousness. "That's right! And don't hurry processing him. The asshole needs to hang with us for as long as possible, give his poor mistreated family a chance to bolt."

Not quite understanding, but unwilling to argue with authority, the younger of the two cops took his time hand-cuffing the criminal, letting him fall as often as he wanted on the way to the police vehicle. Meanwhile, his partner sat comfortably with Maya, ordered a cup of coffee and wrote out the particulars for the arrest.

"Lots of tourists today, Maya. Looks like we'll be in for a busy season."

"Bill, as long as they come to see the sights, I'm fine with it. The lawbreakers here on business are something different altogether. Have you heard any word on the street about the Mosleys selling a new product?"

An older cop, knowledgeable and hard-working, Bill was all ears. His stern gaze held hers. "What kind of a product?"

"New girls. Lots of them. Mostly Filipino. All under-age, and all selling for big bucks."

"I thought we'd cleared out that kind of business long ago. Don't tell me they're at it again?"

"Looks like that particular gang intends to make a splash, earn some big money and feed the animals who can afford to pay for their innocent prey."

"Bloody shit never stops, does it?" Bill slapped the table and then used it to help him gain his feet, his knees cracking more than once. "I'll keep my ears open and get back to you if I hear anything." Sluggishly, as if he carried the weight of the world on his back, he shook his head and sauntered to the waiting patrol car.

In the meantime, Maya scanned the area, hoping against hope that the clone of her missing partner would return. Strangely, she'd believed the stranger who'd sat across from her today. There was a warm aura around him that glowed like the sun with orange streaks. Her instinct to trust had shocked her. After all, that had been one of the problems she'd had with Max.

She'd always known he was number one in his world. But as much as her partner drove her insane, she did care about him. Plus, she needed those files that Max had gone after the last time she'd seen him. The files that held proof that a cargo of underage girls had arrived in their city and, at the moment, were being forced into prostitution.

The last message Max had texted was that he had a good lead, was on it and would have the information they needed to move in. She'd never heard from him or seen him since.

Now what worried Maya was that if there was one shipment, most likely by now there'd be more.

Chapter 7

"Stop crying, Kanya. No one has heard your sorrow except those of us who are locked in here with you. Nobody will come. We are doomed."

"Yes, please have mercy and stop those incessant tears. They haven't helped us, and neither has the screaming for help. You're just driving the rest of us crazy."

Kanya whipped around to the complainers, her temper flaring. "Can't you understand? I don't want to be here. Father and Mother will be frantic, my grandmother is old and my disappearance will kill her. How can I live with that on my conscience?"

In the dim lighting, Malee, the oldest girl of the group, crawled to Kanya and took her hands. "Please my friend, don't blame yourself. This is not your fault. We've all been kidnapped against our will."

Solada, the youngest at thirteen and the prettiest of the girls, spoke up for the first time in twenty-four hours. "Malee, what will happen to us? We know we're on board a ship and it's been sailing for two days—"

"No, no, Solada. We were drugged. Who knows how

many days they kept us here before we regained consciousness? We could have been traveling for a week or more—" Tears were still noticeable in Kanya's voice.

Malee cut in, not wanting to alarm the fifteen girls who were sprawled around the floor on bare mattresses. She was the undisputed leader, not only because she was the oldest at sixteen, but also because she was sensible and strong and her caring attitude made the girls feel protected. Because of this, they allowed her to distribute the food and water and, most importantly, whenever one of them lost control, the hugs. That had frequently happened in the beginning. But not so much now.

Most of the shattered, weary girls just wanted to get out of their stinking, dark, container-prison and face whatever was waiting for them at the end of their horrific journey.

Except they had no idea what to expect, but Malee did. She'd heard the rumors about other missing girls in her village. How they'd been forced into prostitution. Or made to do hard labor for families who kept them prisoner. Her brothers had warned her not to be alone on the streets.

If only she'd listened...

Chapter 8

Because of his disappearing stunt, Nik knew he'd be in trouble with Maya the next time he saw her, but he had some hard thinking to do. And he couldn't do it when her green eyes were scrutinizing him, demanding the truth. He'd never known anyone else who had the ability to drill a message in with their eyes, but those emerald sparklers held such power; they messaged, *don't even think of bullshitting—just don't.*

Not a born liar, telling fibs didn't come easy for Nik. Hell, he'd never *had* to lie before; that skill wasn't in his makeup. His old man hadn't cared enough about what he did, so lying to him hadn't been in the cards. And once he'd left the Bastard behind, he'd been his own man. Even during his SFT—special forces training—and all through his deployments overseas, he'd been straight-up, a man who stood by his word, a strong believer in a certain type of conduct.

After living with a phony scumbag for the first part of his life, his fear that those genes would appear in him had kept him rigid in his personal rules of behavior. Which could be why his men had so much respect for Lieutenant Commander Baudin, that they followed him any-where—some to their death. And it was also the reason Nik had state-sided himself. He couldn't trust his reactions any longer. They were skewed now, abused by the PSTD that plagued him mercilessly.

Acting the part of someone else—an estranged brother he never knew—would be a huge feat for him. Except that he'd made a promise and he knew he'd procrastinated long enough. Becoming comfortable with all the lies that would entail was leaving him anxious and unsettled, but the time had come.

The deal Max had talked him into wasn't going to go away. He knew it. They'd agreed he'd get a lot more information from inside the FBI field office than on the street. And the only way to do that would be as Special Agent Maximilian. Making up his mind, he figured he'd visit Nellie the next day—he still couldn't get used to thinking of her as his mom—to find out more about his brother's history.

As he passed O'Reilly's, a fun bar, he decided he'd better grab some dinner rather going to bed hungry. Feeling comfortable in the air-conditioned bar, he found an empty spot in a booth and ordered a Guinness.

He checked his surroundings and enjoyed examining the old wooden bar, an array of glasses and liquor bottles highlighted by the huge mirrored wall and the hundreds of unusual mugs hanging from the ceiling. Cool yet quaint–a real tourist draw.

The heat had become brutal over the last few weeks and Nik enjoyed the coolness inside. Just as he received his big platter of Irish stew, a commotion from the street caught his attention. A short dude had pranced—no other word for it—past a group of drunks and they'd stopped him. Riled up with liquor and bad behavior, they started pushing him around, playing with him like he was a ball they could throw from one person to the next, only to be roughly shoved once again.

Hell, even if the victim wanted to defend himself, the twisted idiots were making it impossible with their relentless rowdiness. Not liking this crap, Nik began to head out the door, to get involved and put an end to the nonsense. By now, the revelers were having so much fun that they'd accelerated their rough playfulness to assault. Losing whatever common sense they possessed, their teasing had turned vicious and fists and feet were their weapons now.

Within a few minutes, Nik had taken control. Hard shoves to scatter the majority, a powerful backhand to the idiot who didn't want to end his fun, and a threat of calling the cops ended the confrontation. By this time, the poor sucker, who never knew what had hit him, lay in a pool of blood, cuts on the back of his head making most of the mess.

Nik picked him up and hauled his ass into the restroom at the bar, letting the waiter know not to touch his plate. "No problem, sir. I can warm it up for you when you're ready. Be glad to. And a fresh glass of beer will be waiting for you. Man... I never saw anyone move that fast." The white-shirted, apron-clad fellow shook his head and rushed over to the bar where the rest of the customers were recounting the happenings they'd witnessed through the bar window.

Nik supported the shorter guy, his own six-feet-three-inches towering over the now recovering victim. "Hey, quit trying to hit me. I'm the one who stopped the others.

Come on now, settle down." Wrapping his arms around the smaller man soon stopped the nonsense. "Calm down. You're safe now. They're gone."

"Where am I?"

"In the restroom of O'Reilly's. It was the closest place."

"Sure, n' I know what you've got on your mind and the answer is...hell no!"

Chapter 9

In a flash, Nik dropped his arms and let the other guy fall to the floor. "Are you fucking kidding me? Man, I just saved your life."

"Which doesn't give you the right to think I'll repay you with my body." Scurrying on his knees in retreat, the bleeder finally hauled himself up using a sink as leverage.

"Your body? Repay... *Repay?* What the hell are you talking about? I don't want anything from you—certainly not your skinny a—! Jesus, some people are nuts!"

Nik backed off, his hands out in front as if warding off a scary image. He grunted and delivered a few more mumbled curses before he stormed from the room, heading back to his table where the steaming platter and admiring glances awaited.

Shaking his head, he was astounded that he hadn't lost it altogether in the bathroom with that freak. Imagine! The little twerp thinking he was after payback. Unbelievable! *Crazy people...*

"I'm sorry, man. I get all kinds of—"

Interrupting the apology from the long-faced idiot,

Nik growled, "Get away from me."

"Hey, I wanted to thank you."

"You're welcome. Now fuck off."

"Well, you don't have to be like that about it. It was an honest mistake."

Nik glared at his follower and, for the first time, noticed the dude's outfit: skin-tight jeans—the one style of today that he couldn't stand—topped with a short-sleeved silky white shirt buttoned half way to show off a tattooed chest that was surprisingly muscular. The younger man's blond hair was too well kept to be natural, especially after the ruckus he'd just endured, and Nik thought he could smell the faint odor of a hair product, like the kind he'd noticed on some women.

The waiter approached, holding out a wet, white towel and a purse-like shoulder bag and handed them to Nik's pest. "I think this is yours, sir. I remembered seeing you carrying it before those wackos attacked you."

"Thanks, man. How sweet! I totally forgot about it."

"No wonder. Those animals were vicious. I'm glad I noticed it."

"Me too."

The waiter passed over the white cloth. "And this will come in handy to clean off the blood."

Taking the rag, the nuisance swiped it over the back of his head, down his chest and over the arm where dried blood still appeared. "I'm just *so* upset at having to deal with, first, being violently attacked, and then making a huge error in judgment and accusing this hero of a—"

"Look, could you hold this love fest anywhere else but here. I'm trying to eat in peace and you two are putting me off my food."

"No problem, sir. How about I bring this poor fellow

a bowl of stew, on the house, of course, and he can thank you properly?" With a suggestive wink at Nik's nemesis, the waiter rushed to the kitchen.

"Hey, come back here!" Nik yelled in the direction of the departing employee and swore when he didn't get any attention. Next he turned his fixed stare onto the annoyance, who was making free with the other side of Nik's booth. "Go away." Nik's tone brooked no rebuttal. And his accompanying glare would have sent every one of his men fleeing in all directions.

However, it had no effect on the intruder. "If you don't mind, I'll just stay here with you in case those horrible brutes are waiting outside to finish me off. I don't know why some people feel that pounding the bejesus out of a poor fellow minding his own business seems acceptable. You were the only person who stepped forward to help me."

"Hell, I'm sorry I bothered. Look how you repaid me, accusing me of... Bah! I'm outta here." Nik shot to his feet and pulled his wallet from his back pocket. Dropping a couple of twenties on the table, he headed for the door.

Before he could make his escape, the annoyance whipped in front of him and held up the money. "Your dinner is on me. Please. I'd like to show my appreciation."

"No." Nik did an about-turn and headed up the street in the opposite direction, thinking to lose his shadow. Not so easy when the other person acted like a large dab of crazy glue. "For chrissake, leave me alone, will you? Go home."

"I can't."

Fed up, Nik turned on the smaller man and shoved him against the wall. His eyes shooting lasers into the widened brown eyes of the other, he gritted his teeth, took a huge breath and asked the question he knew he shouldn't. "Why the *hell* not?"

"They kicked me out. Kept all my stuff. I managed to take my bag with me, but they've stolen everything else."

Nik's chin dropped to his chest. He inhaled a huge breath to calm his raging temper. Finally, he spoke—slowly, enunciating each word carefully. "Then *go to the police.*"

"I can't."

That did it! Feeling like he was talking to a babbling idiot, Nik lost it and yelled. "Why the fuck not?"

"Because it was the police that took my stuff."

Chapter 10

Maya finally broke down and did something she'd sworn never to do again: she went to Max's house. The last time she'd approached Max's mother, Nellie, about his disappearance, it had been a disaster. The woman had shrieked, slid to the floor and left Maya feeling terrible for having shaken her world to such a degree that she'd collapsed.

Not wanting to put the nice lady through another incident like the last time, she'd purposely stayed away. Hell, until they found a body, they had no evidence Max was dead. Surmising anything at this point could drive a person crazy. He could have decided to take off; that was not likely, but without proof of wrongdoing, other than filing a missing persons report, his disappearance had languished under more critical and current cases. Sadly, there was never a shortage of those.

On her own, Maya had continued with the search to find her missing partner with zilch to show for all her efforts. It was like he'd disappeared into thin air. His apartment had been left in its normal state—bed slept in and unmade, his personal gear spread everywhere, and the contents of his fridge, consisting of orange juice, oranges, beer and white wine... oh, and a few condiments, looked normal. Seems like her partner had a fetish for vitamin C and alcohol.

His stylish suits, of which he had many, were all arranged on one side of the walk-in closet while the casual wear took up a smaller opposite space. Also, his personal paraphernalia like razor and toothpaste, hair gel, and dryer were still scattered around the bathroom, just as they should have been for a person without any plans of leaving. Truthfully, it had looked like the man had left for work and just never returned.

Approaching the front door of one the prettiest homes she'd ever been in, Maya swallowed and reached for the bell. Before it could ring, the door swung open and Nellie appeared, hopeful smile in place, her astonishing blue eyes shining.

"You've found my Max? Maya, tell me you've had some news. He's not dead. I'd know."

Fearful of Nellie's reactions, Maya reached out her arms before admitting that they hadn't heard a thing. When the older woman began swaying, Maya stepped into place to catch her and it was a good thing she did. Nellie's instability increased and her knees gave way.

Maya held her upright and guided her to the plush porch swing before she went down fully. "Here, Mrs. Foster. Sit here and take a deep breath. You might like to put your head down between your knees for a few minutes."

With her arm, Nellie wiped away the moisture pooling on her forehead. "Don't patronize me, young lady. If there was any way I could stop this ridiculous habit of fainting, I would do so in a heartbeat. But, due to an earlier injury, it's not something I can help. Bear with me for a few seconds, let me catch my breath and I'll be fine."

"I was worried my appearance would upset you, and I was right. I'm so sorry. But I need to ask you a few more questions about Max."

"No, I haven't heard from him in weeks and no, I don't know where he is. The last time I saw him, he brought his brother home and introduced me to a son I thought long dead."

Whoa! That must have put you on the floor! Not saying her thoughts out loud didn't stop a fleeting grin before Maya could wipe it off. However, the canny woman saw it and nodded.

"I was out cold for longer than a few minutes, I can tell you. I remember coming to and looking at a man who wasn't Max, yet was his double. I didn't want to wake up in case I'd dreamt the image. You don't seem surprised by my announcement?"

"I'm not. I'll tell you why, but you go first."

Nellie seemed lost in a world of her own, so Maya leaned forward to pat her hand and prompt. "You saw the stranger too? Max's lookalike?"

"Yes, that's what I'm trying to tell you. Except he isn't Max's lookalike, he's Max's identical twin brother, Nik Baudin. When they were babies, people—except for me that is—couldn't tell them apart. Other than different clothes and haircuts, it's still the same today. They're identical down to that one dimple on the right cheek."

"I don't understand? How come Nik doesn't live with you and Max?"

Nellie pointed at the other side of the swing and reached over to the nearby table. She produced two beautifully-painted fans and passed one to Maya to ward off the debilitating heat. Once comfortable, both women leaned back against the light-colored seating, pushed the swing with their feet and fanned the air.

Nellie seemed to be gathering her thoughts. Finally, she began. "Nik wasn't with me because I had been told he was dead. You see, Max and I were fleeing from an abusive situation with my ex-husband while Nik was being cared for in the hospital where the Bastard had put him."

"Hold it! You mean your ex physically abused him? How old was Nik?"

"The boys had just turned two." Nellie proceeded to share the circumstances of her escape from one form of imprisonment to the next. "So we ended up here. Since I was completely devastated by Nik's 'so-called' death, and we had nowhere else to go, we came here to live in New Orleans with my sister and her husband. Another bastard who'd obviously lied to me, and who is probably in hell chuckling with the devil."

"You weren't happy here?"

"Not at all. I tried to make things the best I could for my boy. But as their personal slaves, they made me—and Max as he got older—pay for our keep. Ha! In the end, we won. Max escaped as soon as he'd finished basic training and was accepted into the FBI. Then, first Ed, and eventually my sister Vi died and I inherited the property."

"And you never remarried?"

"Are you kidding? I didn't trust my judgment and would never take the chance of making another mistake like the first. In fact, I hated Max's father so much for killing my other son that, after my divorce, I reverted to my maiden name and had Nik's changed legally too. I wanted nothing to remind me of the animal I had married."

"It must have been a shock to find that Nik hadn't died. Is he here with you now?"

"No. That's just it. He came that day with Max and then left, promising me he'd return as soon as he'd sorted out some personal stuff. I haven't seen him since. I'd hoped you might have some word about either of my boys."

"All I can tell you is that Nik is fine. I saw him yesterday in the market and he seemed well. My problem was that I thought he was Max, and I was furious with him for disappearing."

"Oh, he's nothing like Max. He's hard and bitter, has a lot of ghosts, just like his mom."

Maya giggled. She couldn't help herself. Turning to the petite, gentle, ladylike person sitting next to her, she admitted to being shocked. "You? Hard? I can see bitter perhaps, but I would never have described you as hard."

"Aha! But then you don't know what living with the Bastard could do to a person. I got away. Nik had to hang on for another fourteen years before running."

"You mean he ran away at sixteen?" Now Maya was shocked.

"Yes. After putting his father in the hospital. When he told me that part, I laughed, felt happier than I had in a long, long time. Payback is sweet, even if I wasn't there. So you see, he is my son."

"And you don't know where he is now?"

"Actually, I do. He's coming up the street. And a very strange-looking person seems to be following him."

Chapter 11

Since it was a neighborhood filled with heritage homes and tree-lined streets that echoed with the grandeur of generations past, there could be no explanation for the drive-by shooting that ensued.

One moment, Nik was sauntering along, trying to ignore his pesky shadow, and the next a black SUV passed with the windows rolled down, a rifle barrel extended and bullets flying.

He heard a female-like, high-pitched scream from behind, which prompted him to pivot and pull down the screecher whose hands were flapping in time to the stupid dance he performed. At least the dummy had enough sense to hit the ground with him.

Nik tried to push off the frenzied idiot so he could get the license plate, but the bullets whizzing too close convinced him to stay down. Besides, the strangling arms securing him weren't letting go anytime soon. Clamping his hand over the squawking idiot's mouth helped stop the confusion somewhat, but he wished he could have done more. Yet, punching the guy out seemed like overkill.

Screeching tires signalled the end of the attack, but not before Nik noticed a red-headed woman flying out from his mother's yard. *Maya!* She had her gun cocked and sent a few bullets after the fleeing vehicle—all to no avail. It had made its escape.

In seconds, quiet had returned to the street. Pushing away his clinging burden, Nik rushed to where Maya was returning her gun to her holster. "Did you get the license number?" He hoped she had, but knew by her disgusted expression that she hadn't had any success either.

"No. I couldn't see it clearly, too many trees. Did you?"

"Nope. Too unexpected. Why the hell would someone shoot at me?"

"Maybe they took you for Max?"

"Yeah, I thought of that too."

"Has he contacted you?"

"Who?" Nik stalled.

"Who else? Max, of course."

"No, not lately. How did you find out about us being brothers?"

"You're kidding, right? First of all, you're identical. And in case you didn't know, I'm FBI and I have a few resources at my disposal. Other than Max's name change, it really didn't take too long to find out that he had a twin."

Before Nik could answer, more screams erupted from Nellie's veranda. Dropping his head in disgust, Nik swore and then strolled swiftly to the stairs. There he found his new pain-in-the-ass pal holding Nellie in his arms while waving a fan in front of his *own* face and screeching like a banshee. "I think she's dead!"

"Oh, for chrissakes! Give her to me and fetch a glass of water." Nik gently lifted the small-boned woman in his arms and sat with her in the swing. Then he wrenched the fan from the departing idiot and used it to help her return to consciousness. All the while he talked softly, in a soothing voice. "Come on, Mom. Everything is fine. We're all okay. You can come back now."

Maya helped by undoing Nellie's top buttons and loosening her clothing. Soon the color slowly seeped back to the older woman's face.

Maya turned to see the over-emotional dude put a glass of water close to Nik. Hovering, wringing his hands, he waited. "It's all my fault. Those maniacs were after me. Is she dead?"

"Of course she's not dead. She just fainted." Nik's disgust sounded in his voice.

Switching from fear to worry, the skittish guy's expression changed instantly. "Poor sweetie. She's probably terrified. I know I was. If it hadn't been for Rambo saving my ass once again, I just *know* I would have been lying in a pool of my own blood and guts."

Nik glared his warning and the stranger covered his mouth like a child would, using both hands.

When no one bothered to introduce her, she couldn't help but ask questions. "Who are you? A friend of Nik's?"

"Nik? So that's his name. Even though he let me spend the night with him, he refused to tell me."

Nik interrupted sourly. "You didn't spend the night *with me*, you slept on the couch in my hotel room. And...I didn't *let* you." His irritation was evident. "You picked the lock while I was having a shower and hid under the blanket. Hell, I didn't even know you were there until this morning." The disgust on his face was comical.

"And when you did find out, you didn't beat me up or throw me out. You let me share breakfast." Switching his gaze to Maya, the toadying adorer added, "I admit the poor dear wasn't very happy to see me. I thought for a minute he'd have a cardiac arrest. But he didn't get mean and he did let me eat."

Realizing her question had been sneakily ignored, she asked again. "So, who are you?" Maya tried to hide her grin from Nik, the glowering giant whose gentle maneuvers with his mother were paying off. Nellie was starting to recover.

Speaking overly loudly, he answered. "I'm Julian Freed. My friends call me Juli. And you?"

"I'm Special Agent Maya Barnes, and my friends call me Maya."

"And *I'm* pissed... that you two are having a love-fest when my mother is out cold."

"Oh, Nik, I'm not. Just resting my eyes and enjoying being held by my long-lost son." Nellie opened her blue wonders and flashed a smile to all three caregivers. Her gaze stopped at Juli. "I'm pleased to meet you, young man. *I'm* Nellie Foster, Nik's mother."

Chapter 12

Wanting to get a squad car to the address as soon as possible so they could do a sweep of the street, Maya called in the incident. If by any chance someone saw something that could be useful, the uniforms would do a door to door canvas, interviewing the residents and hopefully getting new details.

While she waited for the phone to be answered, she studied Nik. The handsome bastard looked so much like Max. They were identical when it came to their features and hair coloring and those mind-blowing eyes were bad enough to deal with in one man's face but in two? He'd cradled his mom until suddenly, his face paled and his hands begin to tremble.

Hmm... Strange!

Gently, he lifted her to a chair of her own and then bolted into the house. Ending her call, Maya approached the other two.

"Julian—"

"Make it Juli."

"Right, Juli. What makes you think the drive-by was

because of you?" Nellie seemed taken by the younger man and had allowed him to fetch her footstool and a pillow to relieve her back.

"There're some bad guys after me. And the cops are looking for me too. I can't win." Juli hung his head, and his affected sorrow made both Maya and Nellie smile.

Cutting into the conversation, Maya asked. "First, why are the cops after you?"

"Like I told Nik... By the way, he suits that name—"

"Stick to the subject. Cops! Why?"

"Right. So anyway, they want me to tell them what I saw at the nightclub where I used to dance."

"What did you see?"

"Well, that's just it. I didn't see anything, except for a bunch of guys forcing a truckload of young immigrant girls, who looked quite poorly by the way; some had bruises and they were crying—"

"*Ju-li!*"

"...into the basement of the building." Juli held his hands out in front of him as if to ward off her frustration. "That's it. Next thing I knew, one of the big bruisers caught me peeking and came after me. I never ran so fast in my life. That crazy-assed Neanderthal scared the crap... excuse me, Nellie... the poop right outta me."

Nellie nodded graciously. "Crap works for me, it's a good descriptive word and less graphic than shit."

"That's what I thought myself." Juli shared a grin with her. He winked and nodded toward Maya, who really didn't appreciate their childish humor.

"This isn't funny, you two. It's a serious business. What would you say if I told you that those girls had been kidnapped, are all underage, and being forced into prostitution?"

"I'd tell you not to worry about those particular young ladies. They're free. I let them go. Don't know where they are now, but at least those animals don't have them anymore."

"Free? How the hell did you do that?" Shocked, Maya leaned forward to listen.

Fanning himself with one of the fans, Juli's self-satisfied grin appeared before he got serious. "I have a handy Taser I've been forced to use on occasions when fellows get the wrong impression. I snuck back to my room and collected it. Later, when I returned to the building, I just waited until the big truck took off with most of the men. The two bruisers they'd left to guard the girls were pretty dozy from the spiked beer I'd paid big bucks to a waiter pal from upstairs to deliver. I gave it twenty minutes, then I picked the lock, Tased one frisky fool who wanted to stop me, and released the girls. I sent them to a safe house downtown. Not sure if they followed my directions, but they did vamoose. The problem is, one of the guys came to long enough to make me before I tased him again. Now, I suppose, they want payback."

"What's the address to this safe house? I'll check and see if any arrived there?"

Juli pulled his wallet from his pocket and started searching through scads of papers.

Not wanting to waste a minute, Maya went to the entrance of the house and called, "Nik?" Stepping into the hallway, she called again. "*Nik?*" In the distance she heard a door close and never did get an answer to her demand. *Blasted man!* Maya couldn't believe that the annoying jerk had pulled the disappearing act again. One minute he was sitting with them on the veranda, the next he'd split.

Shaking her head, she lifted the mass of red hair off

her neck and twisted it quickly on top, anchoring it with a clip. Then she grabbed the fan away from Juli and, pulling her white, prettily embroidered cotton blouse away from where it stuck glued to her chest, she viciously fanned herself while digesting what she'd been told.

Having no doubt that Nik had overheard Juli's story, she couldn't believe the prick would pull the MIA card again. Torn between wanting to spend her time trying to find her partner, Max, and knowing she had to follow up on this new lead in the Trafficking Case, she chewed on her lip, trying to make up her mind.

"Where's the address?"

Juli had stopped his search.

"Don't have it on me. Must be in my other pants."

Nellie broke into their conversation and aimed her remark to Juli. "Doesn't that just drive you batty? Happens to me all the time. I'm positive I have something and, sure enough, when I go to look for it, it just isn't there."

Juli nodded effusively at the older woman. "I know! It's *so* annoying... "

"Juli! Pay attention." Maya's eyes drilled him, only to get the feeling he was playing her. Glaring, serious in her intent to get to the bottom of the sticky situation, she gritted her teeth and spoke harshly. "You said you stayed the night with Nik?"

"Yes. Had to tidy up the mess he'd left before I could actually sleep. The man's a slob. You'd think the Navy would have taught him better."

"Navy?" Both women uttered the word at the same time. Maya voice ringing with shock and Nellie's filled with pride.

"Yeah! He's a Lieutenant Commander. With the Seals. Served in Iraq. The man's a hero. Got the Silver

Star...What?"

"How the hell do you know all this?" Maya looked over at Nellie, who shrugged.

"Well, it's not like he told me. But I'm pretty handy with a computer and his was sitting open.... Look, I kinda wanted to see if there were any news stories about the girls. But then I got curious. So...shoot me!"

"Hell, not me," Maya said with a grin, ridiculously happy to hear that Nik, the man she'd felt an instant attraction to, was someone she could be proud of. "I'll leave that chore to your friends—the Neanderthals."

Juli's exaggerated screech made her feel slightly better.

Chapter 13

Nik had taken off, knowing that Maya would be pissed. At first that wasn't his intention. All he'd wanted to do was hide his reaction to the adrenaline rush he'd experienced. When the shakes had hit, followed by sickness roiling inside his tight gut, he'd had no choice. Stumbling to the washroom, he'd stuck his head under the tap, relishing the coldness of the water.

As soon as he stood upright, pain slammed into his head and panic clawed at his nerves. Christ, he had to get away. He couldn't let anyone see him trembling like a little girl who'd seen a fat, hairy spider.

Even though he closed the screen door carefully, it still snapped shut with too much noise. He halted and let his head hang to clear his vision. That damned disorder had waned over the last few days and now, at the worst possible time, it had returned with a vengeance; proof he was by no means cured.

Stalking through a backyard and onto an adjacent street, Nik tried to breathe deeply and release the tension. Prescribed sleeping pills had forced his body into numbing oblivion most nights, but he hadn't felt rested, not really.

Good food and exercise had helped, but this latest incident proved he was far from ready to return to active duty. After all, his men depended on him to be in top condition, not screwed up every time he had to deal with a shock or a surprise situation.

Checking his watch, he hailed a cab and decided to take a pill from the unopened bottle the doctor had prescribed for just such an incident. Then, he'd update his brother and see what the hell Max wanted him to do about this new twist.

Sitting in the cab's back seat, Nik went over in his mind what he'd just heard. Go figure that the little twerp who'd been playing stalker could be so useful, and brave. Nik shook his head.

While based in a war zone, he'd seen it time and again. The mouthy soldiers you'd expect to have balls of steel could become the biggest losers, while the ones you thought wouldn't make it two months before having a nervous breakdown, shocked the shit out of you with their courage and determination.

In Julian's case, when faced with flying bullets the guy had lost it. But, in the dark, sneaking his way into danger was another story. Nik wished he could have stuck around to ask the little guy some questions, but he knew he'd have had to get in line behind Maya. Which was the way it should be. After all, she had the badge.

Paying off the driver, Nik headed behind a popular restaurant and up a rickety, wooden staircase to the living quarters above. Before opening the door, he knocked once and then gave another quick one, only to be stopped dead on the threshold by a furious female.

Grabbing the door from his hand, she hissed, "Stop

that banging. Max has finally dropped off. He's been awake all night, fretting."

"I'm not sleeping." A sarcastic voice sounded from the far side of the room. "I was pretending—to shut you up. Let him in."

Nik stepped past the petite blonde whose chip on her shoulder was as noticeable as her striking gray eyes and her natural curls. Charging to the invalid sprawled on clean white sheets and covered in bandages, she railed in fury, "If you did as you were told, I wouldn't have to *babble*, right?"

Max laughed and then coughed. "Aw, darlin', did I say you were babbling? I'm sorry. You're right, I'm a grouch."

Sniffing with indignation, Linda crossed her arms and tapped her right toe. "Don't you think sweet-talking will get you out of trouble. It's taken me weeks to get your sorry ass healed, and I'm not going to put up with any of your nonsense." She turned to Nik who lounged against the doorway grinning. "And you—wipe that smirk off your face. You saw him before. Broken ribs, bruised like a heavyweight has-been after twenty rounds. He needs at least another few weeks in bed to let his broken leg heal. So don't encourage the idiot."

Hands up, warding off her ire, Nik nodded quickly. "You got it... darlin'."

"Oh, you two! I'm fed up with the both of you." The slamming door gave proof of her mood and her exit.

"She gets a mite vexed sometimes. Guess I deserve it. Don't know what I'd have done if she hadn't of taken me in and nursed me, hiding me from the Mosleys."

"Actually, I don't think she was too mad. At least her wink before she slammed the door made me figure otherwise." Nik watched his brother struggling to sit upright and he rushed over to offer a hand. "Let me help you."

"Bugger off. I can do it myself."

"Christ! Now I know why she'd need to get out for a while. You are an asshole, aren't you?"

"Hell, you don't know what it's been like, lying here in hiding, knowing that if they come for me, I'm a dead man. Putting Linda in jeopardy. If it hadn't been for you, fetching me that night and bringing me here, I'd have died for sure."

"Just be glad they didn't crush your cell phone and that you had me on speed dial. By the time I got to you, you were out cold. Who knows how long you'd have lasted, bleeding the way you were. Good thing you recovered consciousness long enough to tell me where to take you."

"Linda and I had something going for a while, couldn't seem to shake her loose. So I banked on her feelings and hoped she'd look after me. The woman owns the restaurant below and can pretty well work the hours she wants to. Seriously, she's been an angel."

"Hell, she'd need to be." Nik went to the fridge and snagged a bottle of water. "Can I get you anything?"

"Did you bring my cigarettes? Is there any beer? I'd give my left nut for a cold one."

"Jesus, bro, you're on all kinds of painkillers and you want to add alcohol to the mix? I don't think so."

"Whoever told you beer is alcohol?"

"Same person who told me you quit smoking."

"Blasted Maya. She's always trying to get me to quit. Refuses to let me light up in the car—"

"And so she should. Why the hell should she breathe in your smoke? And it wasn't Maya, it was Linda. Besides, if I take over your role, there ain't no way in hell that I'll be putting one of those killer sticks in my mouth and sucking in that poison. If you're serious about me taking on your identity, it's gotta be under my rules."

"Actually, Nik, I've changed my mind. Forget I mentioned it. Don't know what I was thinking, asking you to do something so dangerous. Guess I got caught up in the case."

"It's justifiable, bro. I—"

"No! It isn't. They meant to kill me. If I resurface, they'll do a better job next time—on you."

"Hey, I've been taking care of Nik Baudin for a long time and through multiple war zones. Besides, you said yourself, the only way to get this gang is to dig them out of hiding by having them come to finish the job."

"Sure, but next time, they won't do it themselves. They'll hire a hit man."

"What about the incriminating proof you gathered on their business activities? They took it off you that night. I need to get it back. I won't be able to that without resources and backup. As a citizen, I have none of those, but as Special Agent Maximilian, I'll be far more covered and protected."

"So you're seriously going in as me?"

"You don't think I can carry it off?"

"Not looking like that, you won't. I wouldn't be caught dead in camouflage pants and a black T-shirt. And lose the hair. Good thing we're the same size. Look, all my addresses are in the black book in the drawer of the hall table at my place. The hairdresser I use—"

Interrupting with a snort, Nik looked how he felt—pissed off. "You want me to go to a friggin hairdresser? Aw, fuckie, come on."

"Sherry's really nice, has big tits and loves to laugh. You'll like her. Besides, she'll make you look just like me.

And, she'll do your nails too."

"What? Next thing I know you'll want me to visit a spa and wear men's perfume."

"Spa's address is in the book, and my cologne is in my top drawer, left-hand side, in the bathroom."

"Shit!"

Laughing, Max added. "Now tell me why you're here. Something went down and I need to know what happened."

Chapter 14

When Maya returned home, she immediately sensed something was out of place. Slowly, with her gun drawn, she began a sweep from room to room, ending in the kitchen where she found her perp waiting with coffee and a nod of greeting. "Don't shoot. I'm not armed."

"You're also *not* funny. I could have put a hole in you and there's not a court in the county that would have convicted me. You can't just break into a lady's house and think it's okay. Especially a lady cop."

"I needed to talk to you."

"Ever heard of a phone? Ask for a meeting?"

"I didn't want anyone else to see me. And I sure as hell didn't want to put you in danger again."

"It wasn't you who put me in danger earlier. They were shooting at Juli."

"Yeah. I heard. But we both know that's not true. They were shooting at Max."

"Because they believed you were him."

"That's right."

"How do I know you aren't him?"

"You know."

"Sometimes I do, and then other times... Only one way to find out for sure." Maya stalked towards Nik, moving in between his knees. When he looked up and saw her determination, shock exploded over his expression.

Threading her fingers through his overly-long, black hair, not-so-gently, she raised his face. Her attacking lips stunned him into yielding. She took her time, tasting the lush fullness that had attracted her eyes to that very feature from the first time they'd met.

Breathing hard, she stepped back as far as his hands would let her. "You're Nik."

"I probably shouldn't ask but..."

Breaking his hold, she stared into his narrowed gaze. "When Max tried that eons ago it was a blah kiss, annoying really. I couldn't get away from him fast enough." It was hard for Maya to explain her "knowing" without sounding silly, but often Max's lips were thin with disapproval—one of his least likable traits.

"And now?"

"Oh, baby. If you don't know what just happened, far be it for me to explain."

Pushing, seemingly interested, he continued to dig. "Hey, you attacked me. I want to know." An unholy grin sparked his eyes and, for the first time, Maya saw Nik's lips curl upwards while his face filled with humor.

Smart ass! "Let's just say, from now on I'll never be in doubt which brother I'm kissing." She laughed when she saw the ferocious scowl appear. Instantly, his hooded eyes hid his reaction. Whether he'd felt the attraction or not, she wasn't certain. And she sure as hell wasn't about to ask him.

But the distinct connection zinging between them

couldn't be her imagination. It wasn't possible. The fizzle of awareness was just too precious. From the moment his lips had softened and responded, sweetness had invaded—an emotion she'd never before experienced. But it was one she'd always sensed would make the difference between liking a guy and losing her heart.

Swiping at her mouth with the back of her hand, she wasn't sure if she was trying to wipe him off or save the kiss from fading. Stalking to the coffee maker on the counter, she questioned while sliding in a dark-roast pod and snagging the box of cookies from the cupboard. "Why are you here?"

Chapter 15

Nik crossed his right leg over his other knee, hoping to hide the evidence of his unexpected arousal. Not only was the woman a looker—gorgeous long legs molded by the tight black pants and a mouth the good Lord must have hand-sculpted—she was sexy as hell. With lips that were lush and full, begging to be kissed and pleasure saturating her dazed eyes, he fought for every second of control.

How he'd stopped himself from picking her up to straddle his knees, giving him access to her more delicate areas, he'd never know. Guess the shock of her move had messed with his instincts. Now he'd suffer in silence; no way would he let Maya know just how much he wanted her to come back and lay one on him again. *Shit... it's been too long since I've been inside the slick, wet heat of a beautiful woman's body.* "Have you got a significant other who might be annoyed by that little experiment?"

"Nope! What about you?"

"Not lately." Nik felt the smile all the way down to his erection where rioting sensations still hadn't faded. He held out his paper take-out cup "If you have another one of those, I could use a refill."

Once she had both coffees on the elevated oak table, along with the package of fruit cream Peek Freens, she undid her holster, checked to make sure her gun's safety was secure and slid them both in a drawer of a hallway table. Then she kicked off her medium-heeled sandals and tugged off her black cotton, short-sleeved jacket to reveal a white, sleeveless shirt, which she yanked out of her waistband. The wrinkled bottom of the blouse lay on top of her pants ending at the swelling curve of her sweet little ass. Crossing her arms, she rubbed her shoulders as if they were stiff and her back arched and swayed from one side to the other as if the stretching relieved the kinks.

Finally, he watched as she scooped her shoulder-length, golden-red hair into a mess on the top of her head and hold it place with a large clip. Some of the strands came loose and wispy curls dropped to her shoulders, but most stayed anchored on the top of her head, making her look as cute as... *Hell! Was I really going to add a button? I must be friggin losing it.*

In fact, seeing her without the armor of her job, appearing like any young girl relaxing at home, Nik could feel a yearning come over him. How nice it would be to follow this routine with her every night.

Only, he'd be the one to rub her bare arms and tug the bottom of her blouse out, and then slowly unbutton it to take it off completely. Using his hands and lips, he'd convince her she needed some loving after a hard day's work. The sweet visions made him swallow his coffee too fast and it took him a few seconds to stop choking and coughing... and blushing. *What the fuck?*

Raising herself onto the tall chair across from his, Maya waited until he stopped. Then she settled back and appeared ready for his explanations. Leaning her right elbow on the table to cup her cheek, she chose a couple of cookies and before her first bite, she waved the box in his direction and nodded when he shook his head. "Okay, I'm all ears. What's going on?"

Damn, but this little lady looked good. Hair sticking up every which way, her white shirt with the top two buttons undone, emphasizing her ample curves, and her green eyes sparkling with interest, she waited.

He stared. Couldn't help himself. There was something else hidden in those dampened-down emerald flames. Suddenly, she grinned and allowed him see the sultry passion still simmering. He almost made a move.

No!

He winced. Time to get his mind on the business he was there to discuss.

Observing her expression, his eyes never leaving her face, he started, "I want you to help me play the part of my brother, Max."

"You mean as a special agent?" Compelled upright, Maya no longer looked like a woman relaxed. Now she looked infuriated. "Are you crazy? Not a chance in hell. It's too dangerous."

"Look, I'm a Lieutenant Commander in the US Navy, special forces, black ops. I know my way around anything you guys can throw at me. I've handled more types of weapons than any agent has ever had the misfortune to come up against. Besides, I can take care of myself."

"Well, at least you don't brag."

"It is what it is! I need to find out who hurt my brother. Before they got him, he'd stumbled on some incriminating proof against a gang called the Mosleys and their underground activities, and it goes a lot further than anyone else knows. This file would be all you'd need to haul in the works. I can get it."

Listening, no longer relaxed, Maya asked. "First off, tell me how you know about this evidence, what it is and where?"

"No."

Aggression instantly appearing, Maya stood, her manner assertive. "Excuse me? Do you realize that you're withholding evidence in a possible murder investigation? I can charge you and slap your ass in jail." She wasn't playing games now. Nik liked seeing her assume her professional facade. She was solid, a cop with a purpose.

"We both know you won't. Look, I'm going to play Max, whether you're with me or not." Knowing his next argument was total bullshit, he played it anyway. "I'll go above your commanding officer, Ron Bitters, and probably get clearance. Turns out I have a lot of influential friends in the Navy who would put in a good word for me. But...the fewer that know about me not being Max, the safer it'll be. So, either help me or move out of my way."

"Not gonna happen, Nik. So give it a rest. You don't even look like him. Other than your outward appearance and build, you and your twin are total opposites in personalities and background."

"Not as much as you may think."

"Oh, yes, you are. Look, give me the information he gave you and I promise we'll get those bastards. Trust me."

When the doorbell rang, Maya indicated for Nik to go into her bedroom and wait. She took her gun from the drawer and undid the safety, then she slid it in the back of her waistband.

At that point, Nik hid behind the door and waited to see if she'd need any assistance. But her female neighbor, asking to borrow some milk, convinced him she would be safe. Knowing she'd be pissed, but doing it anyway, he used her balcony, lowered himself to the ground and faded into the darkness.

Chapter 16

"Maya, in my office. Now!" Ron Bitters, Assistant to the Special Agent in Charge in the New Orleans field office, was a powerful man, big and mean-tempered. Thankfully, he had a soft spot for Maya, and though Max got under his skin, he'd acknowledged a few times that, when under pressure, the two together were case-solvers, hard workers, and good agents.

Seeing the flashing streaks of red aura surrounding her irate chief, Maya stiffened her back and smoothed her hair around her cheeks. This could be ugly and she didn't want the man to see her nervousness.

"Yo, boss. Coming." She calmly laid down the pen she'd been chewing on and rubbed her hands over the tops of her thighs. Passing by Becky's desk, one of the other agents working from the same office, she leaned over and whispered, "Remember, I want to be cremated."

"Got it! Can I have your black suede jacket... and those red sandals with the ties and...?"

Maya pretended disgust. "Can ya wait till I'm gone?"

"Not unless I have to." Becky wiggled her fingers while

wearing a cheeky grin.

Maya approached the doorway and watched the irate man fling files from one end of his stacked desk to the other. "Do I close the door for this massacre, or do you want to terrify me in full view of the rest of my suddenly relieved colleagues?" His lips twitched slightly, which gave her hope.

"What the hell is going on with your partner? Is he dead or not? Blasted man pulls a disappearing act like fucking Houdini. Doesn't even have the courtesy to give us an indication of whether he's alive or in a shallow grave in the desert. Has he called you? Have you heard anything lately? Tell me again about the last time anyone saw him."

Now this was kinda spooky, especially after her conversation with Nik last night before the son-of-a-bitch disappeared yet again. Not sure whether to mention the appearance of Nik Baudin or not, Maya stayed in the safe end of the pool. "Nothing's changed from what's up on the board. Last spotted at a nightclub on Bourbon Street. The same one we've had to close down a number of times for prostitution and illegal drugs. When we interviewed the workers there, they all said he stayed about an hour, sitting with a blonde chick. No one recognized her. Then he left, she stayed. Not long after, angry for being deserted, she took off in a huff. Nothing after that."

"And the evidence from the back alley?"

"We found Max's blood, quite a bit of it. Some smudges but no credible shoe prints. The scene looked like more than one goon had a go at him, but we couldn't tell exactly how many might have been there. Of course, as you know, his body was never recovered."

"And no videos or photos of him and the blonde together emerged from any of the other customers, especially of her? You've checked with all the patrons you knew about who were there at the time?"

"Sure. We hunted up as many as we could, and nothing. We've canvassed the streets behind the bar and the lanes leading away, every place within a few blocks radius, and no one saw anything, other than his snitch who gave us zip."

"Useless twit."

"No kidding! I even broke down and went to visit Max's mom, Nellie, yesterday and she hasn't heard from him either."

Threading his hands through his brush cut, Ron lifted an eyebrow and let a small smirk emerge. "Did she drop?"

"Like a rock! Never saw anything like it. Those blackouts must be a real pain for the poor woman."

"Well, knowing Max, I have no doubt the woman was covered with constant bruises while he was growing up. That agent has been a boil on my backside while he worked here, and now that he's gone, he's still damned annoying. You'd think he could do the decent thing and let us find his body so we can put the case to rest. But no... it's just like him to make things ridiculously complicated." Turning his back on her, Ron lumbered over to his chair and sighed with satisfaction as his ass made the seat cushion squeal in pain.

Recognizing his tone for what it was—spewing hot air—Maya kept her mouth shut and the grin off her face. "I haven't given up..."

Bloodshot eyes glaring, quieted her. "Yeah... it's time, Maya. You need another partner. I've let you cruise for far too long. Pulling someone from the day room when necessary worked for a short while, but no more—"

"No—"

"Don't interrupt me!" His bellow and pointed finger stopped her arguments. "It's done. I... What the *hell*?"

Maya turned to see what had made her boss's face turn from red to purple.

Striding toward them with his typical strut, wearing his favorite silk suit and shiny four hundred dollar black shoes, Max made an entrance. He winked first at Becky and then patted the top of her head in the way he knew she hated. In a voice loud enough for both Maya and Ron to hear, he said smoothly, "Hi, Ladybug. I see by your joyful expression that you missed me."

Ignoring the slap aimed at his arm, and Becky's hiss, he moved further into the room.

Bedlam struck the rest of the staff. Most rushed to greet their long-lost colleague. Some leaned back in their chairs, grinning. Everyone had a different way of asking the same question... *where the hell have you been?* Some used crude language while others shared hugs. But the loudest and harshest of the greetings came from the man with Maya who'd shot from his office chair to stomp to the doorway. "Hey, asshole! Get in here. Now!"

Chapter 17

Nik knew he'd be in trouble without Maya backing him up, covering his lapses and, by the shocked anger on her face, she hadn't decided whether she would help him or not. Then he realized the reason why she hesitated. The lady wasn't sure.

Was it him, or Max?

Strangely, he'd taken for granted she'd know him. Guess he looked more like Max than he'd thought. Living as a single child, not being around his twin as they grew up, meant he didn't have the advantage of figuring out how Max would actually behave in moments like these. He had to go by what he'd been taught in the last few hours: what he'd noticed himself since they'd met, use common sense and adlib like crazy. Having it all dumped on him like this, he felt disoriented and weirdly out of his league. And bizarrely hurt that she didn't recognize the man she'd kissed silly the night before.

Not wanting his emotions to show on his face, something he'd never had to worry about as a soldier; he glanced away and saw himself in the window. *Christ, I do look like exactly like Max!* No wonder she was acting strangely. It shocked the shit out of him and he *knew* who he was.

***

Thank goodness, Max had drilled him most of the previous evening and far into the night about all the things he'd need to know to pull off this switch. That is, until Linda had stomped into the room in her bikini-style PJs, and fired both barrels. "Enough, you two! Max, honey, you need your sleep. Remember, it'll be me having to put up with the monster you'll be from the lack of it. So, Nik, go home. Come back tomorrow if you must, but, please, for now, stop!"

Nik looked closely at his double and saw what she had already guessed. Exhausted, Max looked like hell. He'd kept going because he'd known that Nik needed this intelligence. To get away with the switch, he'd need even more. But for now it was sufficient. Worried, Nik headed for the door. "I'm going. Max, take your medication and go to bed."

Ignoring the order, Max continued. "You got the appointment in the morning for the stylist and the spa, right?"

"Yeah, yeah! Fucking torture... ah, sorry, Linda. I mean, freakin' ridiculous as far as I'm concerned." The stubborn glare shot his way made him add, "I know! It's necessary. I'll do it already!" Max gathered his belongings.

"Linda, did you give him the outfit I sent you to get from my apartment? It's what you need to change into after the spa treatment tomorrow."

"He's got it, Max. I told you earlier, remember? Plus, I tidied the apartment like you said. Wasn't much to do, but it's all ready for you to move in whenever you want, Nik."

She tossed him the keys that were on the table.

"Thanks, doll. Tonight, I'll stay at the hotel. But as soon as I look like this ugly dude, I'll head over there and set up."

Max added, "You got the burner phone with my direct dial set up? Use it whenever you need to. I'll have mine with me at all times."

"Yes, sir. Got it, sir." He saluted and chuckled. "Goodnight, you two."

Slipping out the door at the top of the stairs, careful not to trip on the garment bag hanging from his arm, Nik went over to Max's vehicle, flung off the tarp and slid inside. Not fussy about driving fancy wheels, Nik had always preferred a truck. But if he intended on carrying on with this farce, he would have to use his brother's chick-magnet and like it.

He parked a street over from where his appointments would be the next day and made his way back to the hotel. Bushed, he'd approached his room only to stop dead at the open door and groan.

Julian, shirtless, wearing a haughty attitude across his expression and a pair of pink silk playboy shorts that barely covered his bottom, waited, his hands braced on both hips. "So, Nikky! You finally decided it was time to come home."

Chapter 18

"What the hell are you doing here? I told you, one night and then out."

"Sure you did. But you never told me where I'm supposed to go. You know I'm on the run. And you know why. You want me to get shot at again? Maybe next time they'll kill me."

"One could only hope." Nik dropped his armload and headed to the mini fridge for a cold beer. He flinched when he saw the tray of fancy sushi and salads arrayed beautifully. And the chilled bottle of wine. *Well, shit!*

"Excuse me? Do I look like a ghost to you? Maybe I'd like a beer too. Ever think to ask?"

"You want a fucking beer, get your own."

Julian swayed over to the fridge, ignoring Nik's next line.

"I meant buy your own." An *I-give-up* snort followed and a curse came soon after. "I'm amazed someone didn't waste you a long time ago."

Much friendlier, Julian took a swig and then nodded. "Yeah, me too. So, where have you been? Gotta tell you, your lady cop wasn't happy with you. Neither was Nellie. That disappearing act got to both of them." Julian sat on the edge of the sofa, where his blanket and pillow were heaped in the corner with the remote on top. The king-sized bed in the other end of the room still looked pristine. "From what I could gather, you've done it to both of them before."

"Done what?"

"Vanished."

"Yeah, well, a man's gotta do what a—"

"Bull. Those ladies worry about you. Well, one does anyway."

"Mom knows I can look after myself."

"I wasn't referring to Nellie. Maya was pretty upset. She drilled me. Wanted to know what I knew about you. Had me on the hot seat for an uncomfortable few minutes."

"What did you tell her?"

"Nothing important."

Intrigued, knowing that the woman had a very strong presence, the willpower of a mountain climber and the same gift of gab as a slippery politician, he had to ask. "How'd you pull that off?"

"I did what you did. Went to the bathroom and never came back." Julian lifted his beer in Max's direction and, chuckling, Max returned the salute.

Chapter 19

The next morning, Nik purposely left while Julian was still in the bathroom. Looking for the garment bag that the pest had hung in the closet, he snagged it and packed whatever personal stuff he figured he'd need into his backpack and then slipped from the room. Yesterday, deciding not to vacate the place altogether, he'd paid for a month's rent.

Hell, if the little guy wanted to hang out there, he really didn't have a problem. In fact, he figured Julian's knowledge might come in handy down the road. The pesky stalker could take him to the nightclub where he'd last worked and released the kidnapped girls. But that all had to happen after his transformation to Special Agent Maximilian.

Heading in the direction of the spa where his appointment time with the hairdresser loomed, he checked his surroundings, only to see the pain-in-the-ass he thought he'd left back in the room. How the little poser had caught up so fast, he'd never know.

"Thought you'd pull your vanishing stunt again."

"You've got to be kidding me." Not impressed, Nik glared at his sidekick. "Why are you following me, Julian?"

"Juli."

"Juli's a girl's name. Quit changing the subject. Why did you come after me?"

"Because you packed and left without a word."

"I didn't take everything."

"Looked like it to me."

"Well, I didn't, you snoopy bastard. Look, I'll be away for a few days, but the room's paid for. Think you can survive that long without me?"

"You mean you're gonna leave me all alone to fend for myself?"

"You'll survive." Nik stopped in his tracks. "Don't walk like that."

"Like what?"

"Like you're some kind of a model on a runway for a fucking fashion show is what." Remembering his appointment, Nik whirled away from Julian and stepped up his speed. He swore when Julian rushed to catch up, his hips swaying worse and his hands keeping time.

"I do not."

"Yeah! You do. And I don't like it. Either walk normal—stop swinging your hands all over the place—or go walk on the other side of the street."

"So now you're embarrassed to be seen with me?"

"That's not what I said, and don't put words into my mouth."

"I guess you want me to walk like a man." A faint jeer could be heard in Julian's voice. "Like you?"

"What the hell is wrong with the way I walk?"

"Oh! Nothing. Nothing at all. You have a really sexy ass and the way you move it makes me swoon—you should be fined for incitement."

In a flash, Nik had Julian up against the brick wall of the drugstore they were passing. "You keep your squinty eyes off my sexy ass, or *your* ass will be in a sling from the swift kick I plant there. Understand?"

"Hell yes! And just so you know, the way you have of being able to move like greased lightning is *such* a turn on... okay! Forget it." With his hands held up in surrender, and an unholy twinkle in his eyes, Julian added, "I'm sorry, man. It's just so damn easy to yank your chain."

Eyes narrowed, warnings flashing, Nik ground his teeth and watched Julian's eyes register. No way could he ever let the little twerp know that it was his way of stopping the laughter that the little shit had the ability to rouse in him. He'd never met anyone so unintimidated, and who seemed to have complete faith in the fact that Nik was all bark and no bite.

The truth was that he had bitten many in the past, part of the job. Pushed too far, he could and would again. But certainly not the little fellow whose eyes held only worship and warmth.

Shaking him loose, Nik went to pick up his garment bag and dropped backpack, just as a crazy teenager on a bike swooped past and snagged the strap. Peddling for all he was worth, the kid headed up the street with Nik giving chase. He'd have caught him too, but Julian, having taken a short cut through a restaurant yard, materialized on the street where the biker showed up. Leaping from the top of a parked car, Julian dumped the bike and began playing tug of war with the rider.

"Give that back." Stubbornly, Julian held on.

Aiming his fist for Julian's face, the teen's jaw dropped when his opponent's arm blocked the swing. He was even more shocked by the fancy defense moves when he tried to pull Julian down.

Fury etched on a face not yet shaving, the loser looked up to see Nik fast approaching. Shoving the bag sideways along with his attacker, he hopped back on his bike and took off, legs pumping madly.

Julian held out the scuffed, torn backpack, a proud grin lighting his face. "I got it."

"Yeah, I saw. Thanks, man. Guess we're even now."

"Not by a long shot. You saved my life. I saved your bag. I'd say I'm one up."

Nik cracked. He couldn't help the chuckle that broke loose. "How do you figure that?" Heading to his appointment double-time, enjoying Julian trotting by his side, trying to keep up and still perform his asinine wiggle, Nik had to ask.

"Easy. If you're dead, you don't need stuff."

"You're one crazy dude, you know that?" Not getting any answer, Nik turned to his escort. Shocked, he realized he'd been walking alone, talking to the air. Scanning the street, he saw a black SUV heading towards their corner and no sign of the pest. *Talk about a vanishing act!*

Chapter 20

Later in the day, still smarting from the uncomfortable time spent with the boss, Nik followed close behind Maya as she headed towards their area and her piled-high desk. "You're lucky Bitters didn't throw your sad ass in jail for taking a leave of absence without permission, Max. And I wouldn't have blamed him. I know you fed him that bullshit about being kidnapped and escaping yesterday, but I don't buy it. Seriously, where the hell have you been?"

Maya watched Nik's eyes narrow and those sexy lips of his tighten. When he clenched his mouth, the smile lines on each cheek deepened and one side dimpled. Mind you, on a face plastered over with scowls, one couldn't mistake those grooves for anything but signs of anger.

Good! He's mad. The asshole had pulled his stunts too often for her not to want to get some payback.

Just then, Henry Lassiter, Max's favorite drinking buddy, grabbed Nik in a bear hug and gave his back a pounding. "Hey, Max, good to have you back. Gotta tell you, man, ever since you disappeared, Maya has been hitting the streets like a crazy person. She's driven us a mad, working every angle, calling in favors, paying off snitches. And all for nothing. It was like you'd disappeared in a puff of smoke. We'd about given you up for dead."

"Hey, Lassiter, how're you doing? Gotta admit, as ugly as you are, you're still a sight for sore eyes." Nik allowed the familiarity with discomfort and forbearance.

"You too, man. Tonight at the place, the drinks are on me."

"You're on. See you after nine." Before Maya could drag fake-Max from his co-workers, they all stepped up to welcome him back. Damn fool was liked by most in the office... there was something about his expectations that others automatically fulfilled.

She'd finally reached her breaking point. "Hey, big shot, maybe you'd like to try and get some work done? It's why we're here, why they pay us." Maya's biting tone didn't surprise anyone. They were used to her caustic, dictatorial treatment of her partner. How many times had they seen her nose to the grindstone while Max threw wadded-up papers into a wastebasket, declaring it was his way of concentrating?

Nik, however, wasn't used to being talked to in this manner and his stiffening was seen only by the woman who watched for it. *Yess! Hope I'm getting to you, partner. Now, it's my turn!*

Before Nik fashioned a comeback, Ron roared from the open door of his office. "Maya, Max, there's trouble at the port, Napoleon Avenue Complex. Check the container terminal at the dock. They found a surprise in one of the containers." Pointing at two others whose expressions were hopeful, he added. "Backup. Get moving."

Trailing Maya to where she'd parked their wheels, unlike his brother, Nik said nothing. Normally Max hated her driving. But she'd get pissy if he insisted on taking the wheel. As a hot-headed teen, he'd wrecked a car and put a buddy in the hospital, which had effectively killed the speed monkey that had ridden his back through those early years.

Now, in her estimation, the jerk drove like a paranoid old lady. The reason he owned such a sweet ride, she'd surmised, was for acquiring chicks and creating envy. Whenever he'd be forced to punch it, he clearly suffered every minute his foot rode the pedal.

"So, are you going to tell me where you've been?" Maya swung the wheel hard and headed for the busy street.

"So—are you really going to play this game?"

"Game? Not sure where you're coming from, Max, honey. I just wanted to understand why you left—"

"Maya. Stop. You know it's me."

"Nik? Oh my God, you so had me fooled."

Nik grabbed the handle above his head tightly. His croaked, "Not even for a second," made her laugh. Seems she'd found a sore spot with the hard-ass. He didn't like her speeding either. Good! She punched the peddle down further and took another corner too quickly. Little did he know that she raced at the track on her off weekends. In fact, there wasn't much in the way of wheels that she couldn't drive. One of her crazy step-daddies had seen to that.

"How did you know I'd made you?" Ignoring her, the man stared straight ahead.

Face pale, wearing a stoic expression, he answered, "You stared at my mouth. Then you sneered. Figured you had no reason to be angry with Max. In fact, just the opposite. If you've been searching for him, like the other agents suggested, you'd have been thrilled when I appeared. You weren't."

"What did you expect? You know it's against the law, impersonating an FBI agent, don't you? No way do I want to get the book thrown at me for aiding and abetting. Far as I'm concerned, you're Special Agent Max Foster, and no one else."

"Fine with me. So now, are you going to bring me up to date on what you know about my brother's disappearance?"

"You mean death?"

Peeling his eyes from the road, Nik's head whipped in her direction. And he didn't speak, he barked. *What the hell?* "Did you find him?"

"Not exactly."

For a second, Nik had thought Max had turned up dead since the night before. Why that ridiculous thought had entered his mind, he'd never know. After all, both Maya and Bitters had accepted he could be Max just a short while ago. Daunting was the only way he could describe how much he cared for the brother he'd only recently met. It was like, for the first time in his life, he was whole—nothing missing—complete. Heart pounding fast and suffocatingly hard, he tried to relax.

"I finally found his snitch, and he swears Max was beaten so badly he couldn't have lived through it."

Rigid with instant rage, Nik said, "Hell, if he saw Max being assaulted so badly, why didn't the asshole step in?"

"The guy's an addict, uses every day and has no devotion to anything but the shit he shoots up with. Very little he could have done. Besides, he was terrified they'd kill him too."

"Does he know who did it? Or who took his body?"

"No. He conked out. Says the adrenalin from the panic

did him in and when he came to, Max was gone."

"Strange coincidence, wouldn't you say—that he just happened to be hanging out in the vicinity on that exact night."

"No fluke. He says he'd found some evidence for Max and he needed a hit. Knew Max was good for a twenty, so he'd phoned him. Max had said he'd meet him behind the restaurant, but when the informant showed up, the goons had already started."

"Evidence? What kind of evidence?"

"Wouldn't say. Well, actually, he had a memory lapse. Guess he'd only talk to Max, and nothing I said could sway him."

"Could he identify anyone?"

"Nah! Too dark. Too high. Hell... too stupid." Maya drove through the open gates of the New Orleans cargo terminal and followed the signal from the uniform who was there to direct regular traffic away from the crime scene. The activity around one container appeared to be the place to stop. She pulled up with a screech of tires and a rattled partner.

Goodie! He'd grabbed the dash and held on. Amazing how much better she felt. Until she saw the body...

Chapter 21

Taking the gloves held out by a member of the forensic team, Maya waited for Nik to don his and then walked in front of him to show him the way. Hopefully, he'd be smart enough to follow her lead in these circumstances.

The woman stepping forward to greet her wore a badge and a scowl. Bessy Halls was a good detective and one of Maya's preferred officers to work with. There was no one-upmanship with her. Bessy did her job well, passed in the appropriate paperwork on time and could be relied on to be discreet. A hell of a lot better than many of the penis-porters who were out to prove their size.

As a matter of respect, Maya held out her hand. "Hey, Bess, appreciate the call. What have you got for *us*?"

Bessy smiled a greeting and then spotted the man behind her. "Max!" With a leap of joy, she flung her arms around Nik's neck and swayed back and forth while pounding him on the back as if burping her little one.

Since the beautiful black lady not only wore a large smile but also sported strong arms and a healthy hold, Nik returned the hug and felt foolish grinning in the way he thought his brother might have done. "Hey, gorgeous, I missed you too."

Maya knew she was being silly, but seeing Nik in another woman's arms didn't sit well with her. Muscles tightened in her tummy and let her know that though her reaction had been visceral it had been no less annoying.

Funny thing—Max could have stripped naked and had full blown sex with the woman and it wouldn't have bothered Maya one little bit. Well, other than the annoyance of having to arrest two people she liked for indecent exposure and gross lewdness.

She finally snapped. "Break up the love fest, you two. Appreciate you including us on this one, Bess."

"Yeah, well, I know you're working on the Trafficking Case and I figured this incident was right up your alley."

"Thanks, pal. Show us what you've got."

Bessy grabbed both sides of Nik's face and planted a big smooch on the right-side dimple that was now prominent. "Sugar, you're a sight for sore eyes. We'll have to celebrate your return from the dead later." Her expression turned serious and her voice changed, lowered, becoming emotional. "Can't tell you how many times I got called out about a deceased male and worried myself sick it might have been you." With another hard slap on his arm, Bessy swung to Maya and said. "Okay, agent lady, I'm coming." She led the way to the container that had been taped off and stepped inside where lights were set up so they could sweep the crime scene once the ME had done his initial investigation.

The sickening heat hit Maya as soon as she moved in from the entrance. Good Lord! It was hard to breathe in the putrid, dead air. A person almost had to gulp it; the texture was so thick it punished the lungs.

"Hi, Maya. Figured you'd catch this one." Stepping away from the body, the coroner, a bald good-looker swung his appreciative brown sparklers in her direction and winked. Reaching over the covered corpse, he held out his hand and shook Nik's. "Good to see you alive, Agent Foster."

"Thanks, man." Max had primed him well. *If you don't know the name, just use the generic "man." I do it all the time.*

Maya crouched down. "May I?"

"Sure, the MEs have finished with her. They'll transport her to the morgue soon. Wanted you to see the crime scene, though, before then."

"Thanks." Maya lifted the shroud and sat back on her heels, away from the stench. She'd never gotten used to the nostril-pinching stink of death. Or the painful reaction she suffered whenever the victim was young—male or female. For the next few nights, she'd be experiencing reactionary nightmares for sure, and her brief crying spells over these cases had never stopped.

Guess she should be glad that she hadn't become cynical about the heart-rending atrocities. Rather than hardening her like it had so many others, her pervasive streak of humanity demanded she did the best job she could for each victim. Thankfully, her acting skills had also greatly improved. No one knew the gut-wrenching torment she suffered.

Nik coughed, covering his mouth. It drew her eyes to him and she saw that he'd guessed her secret. The flash of sorrow he shared before he'd deadened his own expression had been for her alone. Damned if it didn't make her feel better.

Surveying the body, Maya surmised that the girl couldn't have had her fifteenth birthday yet. Nor could she have been any prettier. *Poor baby!* Maya acknowledged the approaching ME. He'd been waiting to give her the information he knew she'd be asking for.

"Cause of death?" From the look of the shrunken eyes and swollen tongue, Maya had a pretty good idea, but it was best to ask—professional courtesy.

"Dehydration. She might have lasted three days, maybe less, because of the heat. From the look of the shriveled, irritated skin, the poor girl suffered until ketosis kicked in and her kidneys and other organs began to fail."

"Yeah, that's what I thought. Looks like she did a number on her arms and legs, scratched herself bloody raw." Sadness threatening, Maya forced it back as usual. She couldn't afford to show her reaction. Not yet. Not here.

"She did." Nik had wandered to the other end of the container and pointed to the wall near where the young girl had made herself a nest of old papers and scraps of wood. "She's left a message." He scanned his flashlight over the bottom of the wall where there looked to be distinct letters written in dripping darkened blood.

Maya went to have a look, swaying slightly as she gained her feet. "Can you make out what it says?"

Squatting, Nik aimed the flashlight closer and read the message. "'*Mai 14 help her.*' That's it."

Chapter 22

After taking her own pictures with her cell, Nik saw Maya's gesture that she'd gotten everything she needed. Earlier, the temperature had registered ninety-five in the shade, humid as hell, but he'd never been so glad to go outside.

He'd noticed that Bessy had disappeared, and the rest of the folks working the area were busy. The ME who Maya had called Ray followed them outside. Stopping her with a proprietary hand on her arm that Nik had a primeval urge to break, he asked for a minute.

Easy...Down, big boy!

Not sure what the procedure was, Nik let Maya do the talking while he studied the surroundings. The port looked to be a very busy place. Hundreds of containers, docked ships being unloaded by huge cranes and numerous vehicles crowded onto a small area.

A large eighteen-wheeler caught his attention. Near the back of the now empty trailer walked a heavy-set man. His shifty surveillance of the surroundings spiked Nik's interest. When the nervous fellow rounded the corner of the warehouse, he stopped dead, his eyes widening from seeing all the cop cars and uniforms bustling around.

Nik sensed something amiss and began to move in the fat man's direction. Seeing the agent approaching, the prick's face registered first fear and then panic. Quickly, swinging back in the direction he came from, he headed for the driver's side of the truck and Nik's instincts kicked in.

Pushing himself hard, he made it to the vehicle just as the idiot had started the engine and begun to swing the steering wheel. With a leap that he'd perfected in basic training, Nik reached through the open window and grabbed hold of the wheel. With Max's Luger pressed to the other's cheek, he forced the runner to make a decision—gas or brake. "You better stop right now, fuckie, or your pea brain will be plastered all over the windshield." The gun, held by an unbending, hard-eyed Nik, convinced the lowlife that his best choice was to stop.

By the time Nik had flung the quivering, whining sack of shit from the interior and had him on his knees, Maya had run up, followed by the few others. "Get down on the ground. Hands behind your back. Do it! Now!" Her voice snarled the commands before Nik had a chance. Good thing. He had no idea how to give the correct orders to a fugitive. Seems that Max hadn't covered everything.

Turning to him, Maya grinned. "Good work, Agent Max."

Obviously, there was a message in her words. The others snickered. But he had no frigging idea why. Another thing Max had left out.

Chapter 23

"You did good today, *Max*." Maya drove slowly back to the office. Nik snorted and glared in her direction. She knew very well who he was, and, for some strange reason, he disliked her calling him by his brother's name.

"Don't get pissed." Maya's voice softened.

"I'm not." He turned away.

"Yes you are. I can see it in your face. Your dimple is showing from clenching your teeth."

Swiveling back to face her, he grunted. "First of all, I don't clench my teeth. And second—I don't have dimples." The sneer came through loud and clear, even to him.

"Technically, you're right. They're more like laugh lines. Except you never laugh, so they must be there from—"

"When I grit my teeth. You're nuts. Why are you calling me Max when we're alone?"

"If I don't, I'm afraid I'll forget and call you Nik in front of the others. How about I just call you Swift? That was some fast move you made today. I've never seen anyone who can react like you did. Well, there is a certain resemblance to the Road Runner in the Wile E. Coyote films."

Her teasing grin relaxed his stiff demeanor and he replied, "You're crazy. But I see what you mean about forgetting in public. Guess you're right."

"What? A male who agrees with a female? Watch my heart!"

"Don't get too used to it." He grinned evilly and settled back in his seat. Maybe working with the red-headed darling was going to succeed better than he'd thought. He hoped so. Until Max was strong enough to be able to defend himself, and he took up his rightful place, it would be better if he remained in hiding. Considering how Nik had had to use strong-arm tactics to get his stubborn twin to agree with this exchange at all, he'd had to let him call some of the shots. When they'd argued about telling Maya that Max was alive, Max had negated that suggestion instantly... and forcefully. "Bad enough that she'll be culpable for you acting as an agent and could lose her badge for playing along. But if she knew I was alive, she'd be even more prone to call it in. That woman plays by the book."

Interrupting his wanderings, Maya questioned. "How did you know the truck driver had something to do with the dead girl?"

"I didn't. But he looked mighty guilty when he saw all the cops and police vehicles. When he ran for his truck, I just knew I had to stop him and talk to the dude."

"You have good instincts. Your perp, Al Bard, has a list of misdemeanors a mile long and has been incarcerated a number of times—mostly vandalism, hauling stolen goods and drug possession. The fact that he had a bag of cocaine in his shirt pocket and a couple of stolen guns under his seat gives us leverage. He's looking at some hard time if he doesn't talk."

"You sound gleeful."

"I am." She chuckled and he liked the sound.

"Who'll be interviewing him?"

"We will. They're booking him and taking him to the field office."

"Ah! That's why you're happy. You get to intimidate the poor bastard."

"That poor bastard could have had something to do with our young girl being left to die all alone in that furnace with no food or water. Yeah, you bet I want to talk to him."

Nik heard the pain in her voice and zeroed in on her anger. "You care too much. It must rip your heart out every time you come up against a case like this." He waited while she made up her mind whether to trust him or not. He glanced her way and saw her bite down on that lush bottom lip that caught his eye more than he liked. Fantasizing about how sweet it had tasted during their kiss drove him wacky and he wished he could get her taste out of his head.

She took a deep breath that ended in a weepy sound and it went straight to his heart, tore a large gash through the middle, and left him yearning to cuddle her closely.

Words seemed to break loose of their own accord. "Some nights I can't sleep. The victims won't stop haunting me." Her voice had lost its teasing quality and had become somber and sad... and hesitant. As if she didn't know why she was sharing but had no choice.

He was glad she did. And to acknowledge her lowering her boundaries, he decided to pay back in kind.

"Me too! I can't stop seeing the shattered bodies of three of my men who'd followed me into a mine field. I made it through and they didn't, and I'll never know why. One wrong step..." His voice broke and he shut up.

Reaching over from her side of the car, she slid her hand inside of his and smiled when he squeezed tightly. "Two night wanderers with nightmares. Call me anytime that they won't give you peace."

"Works both ways." He cleared his throat and was glad to see the parking lot as they pulled into their slot.

Chapter 24

"What do we do now?" Nik scanned the forms that Maya threw across to him. "What're these for?"

"I got this info from the FBI data bank. Read it over and search out: Al 's last known address, girlfriends, employer, places he likes to hang out. Whatever we have on him is there. I'm going to see if those videos I requested were sent over from the dock and whether the IT guys have found anything yet."

"Will they have them for the last few days?"

"The manager said their equipment is faulty. He's sending over everything they have, but he doesn't hold out much hope that we'll find a lot of decent footage."

"Can I go in with you when you interrogate Mr. Bard?"

"Of course, it would look weird if you didn't. By the way, partner, you have an uncanny ability to tell when someone is lying, and a good sense of when to break into the conversation. If you get the irresistible urge to do your thing, feel free. Otherwise, let me handle the bastard." Nik heard the warning and had full intentions of following Maya's advice. No way did he want to obstruct their chances of obtaining credible intelligence.

***

An hour later, Maya waved for him to follow her. "They've got him set up in one of the interview rooms and we're good to go at him now. Did you find anything useful?"

"Not much. The guy's a loser. Supposedly, he just started working for the trucking company, Smith & Sons. I called their office for a lowdown. I think we should check them out."

"Why, what happened?"

"They weren't too forthcoming on the phone, said they'd never heard of Al Bard. Their truck had been stolen that morning and he was most likely the thief. I did a run-down on their business. Found some discrepancies."

Maya stopped and turned to him. "How did you get into the computer?"

"I didn't. Got Ladybug to do it for me." He smiled with a wicked glint in his eyes that made Maya laugh.

"I'm not even gonna go there. How you men get that poor girl to do those 'little chores' for you all the time, I'll never know. Anyway, what did you find out?"

"The old company, New Orleans Shipping, sold last year to Smith & Sons, who've lost a lot of business ever since. Doesn't seem to be affecting their bottom line, though. Makes a person wonder how they're staying alive in the competitive world of shipping and long-distance hauling. I think we should pay them a visit."

"Sounds like a good idea. First, we'll talk with the perp and see if he knows anything about his so-called employer, as well as the dead girl."

"Have they identified her yet?" As they traveled the long corridor of the brightly-lit office, they carried on with their conversation.

"Interpol is searching now. Because the container arrived from Singapore, we're sure she came from either Thailand or the Philippines, their favorite hunting grounds. Those two countries are a haven for human trafficking. From there, it's easy to gather shipments of girls for either sexual or labor exploitation. If a market has now been set up in the U.S. for those poor young women, the dudes we're talking about would have no compunction about hiding them in containers and shipping the merchandise overseas. All they need are connections placed in strategic places to facilitate the process."

"So you're sure she traveled to the U.S. in that container?"

"Not necessarily. We know she spent days in there from the crime scene investigation, but it doesn't prove she arrived in that same container. In fact, from the condition of the inside, I'd say it wasn't likely. Unfortunately, we got next to nothing on those surveillance videos. Almost looks as though they've been tampered with. The port authorities, with the help of some of our people, are looking into it now. Anyway, I'm hoping that our friend, Al Bard, can tell us more about her story."

Nik added, "My thoughts are about Mai, who's only fourteen." Those words written in blood had haunted him ever since he'd shined his flashlight on them.

"Me too. God... I hope we can find out more about where she might be now."

"You think this idiot will know?"

"We can only hope. Not only that he knows, but that he'll share. If I can get him to care more about saving his own ass than his boss's, maybe we can find out."

Chapter 25

Loaded with questions, Maya stepped into the interview room followed by her partner. Unknown to Nik, Max had played this game with her in the lead many times and they'd worked it well together. They'd both understood when the other needed to take over and when to back off. However, Nik didn't have the experience or the training. It would be up to her.

Before opening the door, Maya warned. "Remember, if you don't know what to say, leave it alone. I can handle him, okay?"

"Got it!"

Glad that he was totally professional about the situation and hadn't taken offense, she went in and placed her papers on the table in front of Al Bard and leisurely sat down.

Arms crossed, Nik stood leaning against the wall near the large mirror. His expression of boredom and disdain were exactly what Maya had hoped for. Before getting into character, she threw him a quick wink to let him know she liked his pose. Then she became the agent everyone in the office recognized. The one who could burrow into a person's psyche and get them to believe whatever she wanted.

Examining the sack-of-stupid across from her, she noted that his aura showed mostly grays and dark hues mixed into various other tones—all pale. This asshole had very little heart and no sympathy whatsoever. Working over this psycho, using a young girl's death as a sympathy ploy, would get her nowhere. Maybe self-pity would.

"I don't know Jack shit about nothing." Slouching against the back of his chair, the idiot spoke up without giving her the courtesy of any other form of greeting.

"Yeah, Yeah! That's a new one to me. Never heard that before, have you, Agent Foster?" As if she had all the time in the world, Maya slipped off the black jacket she wore over a silky, white tank top and slowly hung it on the back of her chair.

***

Nik didn't answer at first until the silence grew and he realized she was eyeing him. It prompted the perp to look his way too, and that's when he saw the fear Al couldn't hide. In fact, he could smell it radiating in waves off the prick. He'd seen it before when his men were expected to go into battle and perform at their best. Some were cocky and had no doubts about their ability. Others acted indifferent so well that you wouldn't know their fear existed without years of experience in working with them. Still, others had a sixth sense that their time was limited and they were coasting on thin ice. That's the way Al Bard looked. Excitement began to sizzle inside him. If they played it just right, they could get this man to spill his guts. His faith in Maya had to hold.

Grinning confidently, he finally broke the spell. "Nope. It's a new one to me."

Smiling back at him, Maya took quite a few seconds before turning in Al's direction. "Hope you had a good time this last week as a free man, Al, because you won't be seeing the outside of a prison cell for one hell of a long time."

Al stared at her, ogled her chest area, his eyes undressing her. She let him see just what he'd be missing.

He flinched so slightly; you had to be watching for it to see the movement. Then his face hardened back to the mask of indifference he'd worn when she'd first stepped into the room. He didn't speak, but now his fingers played a tune on the gray metal table top.

"That sweet girlfriend you've been living with, Sadie Moore, will get herself a new man faster than I can say twenty years. Oh, yeah! She'll be finding herself another daddykins very soon." Maya threw a photograph across the table, showing the face of a younger woman in her twenties with a big hairdo, blue eyes and overly reddened, pouty lips. "We'll be investigating her thoroughly; could be she's your accomplice."

Al glanced down but still didn't reply. His fingers worked the table a little faster than previously.

Deciding to try another tack, Maya switched gears. "Did you know that dead girl in the container you were after was underage, a child?"

"I wasn't after any container."

"Don't be stupid, Al. We got your paperwork. Not only were you there to pick up a container, but it was also that particular one you came for."

"Don't call me stupid!" Al's chin wobbled from the instant anger her words produced. "I didn't know what I was supposed to pick up. I had my manifest and was going to turn it into the loading guy at the dock. Only they knew what I had to collect."

"Well, you're right about that. They knew you were to collect that container, all right. But they swore it hadn't been opened and so there was no way of knowing there was a girl locked inside. The box sat in the cargo area for three days in the sweltering heat, waiting for someone to fetch it."

"I don't know nothing about that." Al crossed his arms and glared at her with righteous fury.

"No? It was shipped from overseas to Smith & Sons, your so-called employer, who, by the way, filed a report that their truck—the very one you were driving—was stolen. Seems they have no record of you being on their payroll either. You do realize, they're going to throw you under the proverbial missing truck, Al. They don't give a rat's ass about your troubles."

Maya grinned gleefully at Nik. "Poor sucker won't even get a paycheck when this is all said and done. Instead, all he's looking forward to is a stretch in jail while his pretty lady friend moves on to another guy."

Nik couldn't help himself. "Hell, now that I know she'll be free, I might just look her up myself. She works at the Pink Pussycat, right? I might need a drink after work tonight."

Without any warning, Al shoved himself away from the table and lunged at Nik. He went for his throat, both hands extended to grip and maul. Problem was, those same hands ended up being used to flip him over onto his back. And it happened faster than either Al or Maya could blink and prepare for.

The pressure from Nik's knee placed strategically across the other man's neck convinced him he'd better stop wriggling. "You going to behave?" Nik stared him down and waited for Al to acknowledge who had the power. Al's nod did just that, and with a move no one expected, Nik lifted him and planted his ass back in the chair.

"You're a patsy, you know that? I sure as hell don't feel sorry for anyone who's begging to be screwed as much as you are." As if he'd touched something that had gone bad, Nik dusted his hands on his pants and returned to his stance by the wall.

"You wouldn't believe anything I tell you." Al had trouble getting the words out through his now raw throat.

"Try me," Maya leaned forward watching Al rubbing his neck, tears forming in his eyes—tears of self-pity.

"I didn't know nothing about no dead girl in the container. All's I know is they lost something and it wasn't until this morning that they found out what had happened—that the cargo was in that container and it needed to be fetched. I overheard them talking when they called me into the office. I don't know nothing about no dead body."

"So you do work for these guys?"

"Yeah, sometimes. They call me for special jobs. That's all I'm saying. I want my lawyer before you get anything else."

Chapter 26

Rather than driving straight to the offices of Smith & Son, Maya and Nik stopped off at a courtyard café for lunch. They shared po'boys and coffee, both anxious to discuss what they'd learned from Al Bard.

"You always strip off your clothes to snare the male offenders?" The cranky way Nik asked made her pay attention.

Her expression lit up with pretend disbelief. "I was hot?"

"So was Al."

"You really got a problem with a girl using every bit of ammunition she can to suck in slime like him?"

"Well, when you put it that way."

"I know a lot of male cops who like to prance around the room, show their muscles, play the ego card. All I did was remind the idiot of what he'd be missing after being put away for a lot of years. Sometimes it works, many times it doesn't. No harm in trying. You sound jealous."

Looking uncomfortable with the knowing smile she sent his way, Nik changed the subject. "Did you read the report on Smith & Sons that came in before we left?"

She nodded and chewed her lunch, her teasing expression changing to utmost satisfaction. "Hmm... my favorite food aside from jambalaya and fried catfish." She licked the sauce from her lips and watched him zero in on her mouth. She almost blew him a kiss and stopped herself just in time. What the hell was she thinking? This man was a virtual stranger. And yet, she instinctively felt more comfortable with him than she ever had with his brother. Watching, she saw him arch his neck one way and then the other as if the gorgeous silk tie he wore was choking him.

"You're not comfortable in Max's clothes, are you?" She wouldn't give him the satisfaction of admitting he wore the clothes better than Max. There was something about the way he relaxed his body... not wound tight all the time. It was sexy, a come-on, one she fought against.

"No! I dislike suits. Even the military dress uniforms are a pain. But the reason I'm not relaxed is because I don't think we should be sitting out in the open like this. After that last ambush, we know the word is out that Max's back from the dead. Whoever worked him over in that alley must be thinking he'd screwed up badly. Most likely, he'll try again."

"You say that as if you know he got out of that alley alive."

"You never found a body."

"That doesn't mean diddly. There're a lot of swamps out there that they could hide a man in and no one would ever find the body."

Nik came close to sharing his knowledge with her. Only his promise to Max kept him quiet. "True. So, if they did haul his body out there, he could have miraculously survived. That means they'll believe I'm him and they'll make doubly sure not to screw up again."

All of a sudden, Maya saw Nik's expression change from a man listening to one sending a warning glare.

Maya, too sharp to have missed this little ploy, turned to see who he was signaling and saw a blonde cook do an about face and head back into the kitchen. *Now what the hell was that all about?* Before she could question him, he changed the subject.

"What's next on the agenda?"

Shrugging, she answered, "I figure we're on to something with Smith & Sons. The information we've got is really sketchy. Seems you were right about their income not resulting from a lot of transporting freight. On the other hand, because they own a shipping company, they get to show up at the docks whenever they have containers arriving without anyone questioning their presence. It's pretty slick when you think about it. With their trucks, they can shuffle the girls all over the country, feed their operations in the major cities and no one is any the wiser."

"What I don't understand is how they get the cargo screened and passed through inspection?"

"That's easy. All you need to do is pay off certain people who're employed in different vicinities. Inspectors, warehouseman, loaders. Actually, thanks to you, we're on it. We've started a huge information-gathering sweep and it's happening right now to the employees who work anywhere that Smith & Sons have contracts. We'll find our link. In the meantime, let's go and see what Mr. Smith has to say. "

Chapter 27

Smith & Sons was a run-down office building inside a fenced-in yard with little activity happening. Also, there were a whole lot of unkempt laborers visible, sitting around, screwing the dog.

Nik had felt uncomfortable from the minute they'd exited their Fed vehicle and entered the premises. Several characters stalked them with steely-eyed glares, and for him to walk nonchalantly alongside Maya took all the acting skills he possessed. His training would have put him at a crouch with a high-powered rifle in his hands and a platoon behind.

Shocked at how toxic the place felt, he could only imagine how the atmosphere affected a woman. Yet, one might think she was taking a leisurely stroll through a Macy's lingerie section. *God, this gutsy chick was getting to him!* Red—no gold—in the sunlight, her curls framed her beautiful face and he had an urge to walk closer, his hand holding hers, tagging her as his property.

For the first time, her slight frame concerned him. He knew she'd be overpowered in a fight, should one break out. Sweat pooled under his collar, not just from the hundred or so degree temperature, but from the instant fear he felt for her safety. Without him meaning to, his hand went to the weapon attached to his belt and it stayed there until they entered the dilapidated building accentuated by dirty windows and weeds dying against the unpainted walls.

In the front office, a tall wooden counter swamped the small space. Behind, at a cluttered desk, a man sat, playing on a computer, surrounded by papers stacked everywhere, mostly covered in grime and dust. The lack of work being done was obvious. As a front for whatever shenanigans they were covering up, the place was perfect.

The skinny, bored clerk, maybe in his early twenties, glanced their way. As soon as he saw they weren't part of the crew, he sat up and swallowed, his protruding Adam's apple doing a dance number in his long throat.

"Can I help you?" At least he spoke with some degree of courtesy.

Maya flashed her badge, and a poke from her reminded Nik to pull his out too. "Good afternoon. I'm Agent Maya Barnes, and this is my associate, Agent Foster. We'd like to speak to Mr. Smith, the owner."

"Do you have an appointment?" The little shit in front of them bleated the spiel he was obviously trained to use. Nik wanted to reach across the disgusting, dirty barrier, grab his scrawny neck and haul his disrespectful ass closer. Instead, he stood back and waited to see how Maya would handle the situation.

"As a matter of fact, this badge says I have an appointment with the man whenever I want it. Now pick up that intercom and tell him Agent Barnes wants a few words."

Running dirty fingernails through short-cropped hair, the idiot hesitated until Nik stepped forward warningly.

Then he did as he was told.

After speaking into the phone, informing his boss about the visitors, he pointed to the doorway on the left and gestured for them to enter.

Nik walked over and opened the door. Once he'd ascertained that one man dressed casually in shorts and a white golf shirt sat with his feet propped on the desk, holding a tablet in his hands did he move aside and let her precede.

Their host laid his toy down and sat up, taking his time to acknowledge their entrance. Finally, he looked at them arrogantly and spoke. "I understand you wanted to see Mr. Smith? I'm Smith junior. My dad isn't here. What can I do for you?"

Nik took an instant dislike to the muscled-oaf scumbag, whose eyes were literally undressing Maya as she pretended indifference.

"We have some questions for you, Mr. Smith." Maya took her time, her husky voice low, making him strain to hear. "You registered a stolen truck this morning with the NOPD, and we've come to inform you it's been located and is being held at the Claibourne impound."

Pretending astonishment, Smith said, "You mean to tell me the Feds are making personal visits to all robbery victims now? I'm impressed by your dedication."

"Well, I'm *unimpressed* with you thinking we'd believe for a minute that Al Bard *isn't* your employee and that you *didn't* send him to pick up that container. You know, the one imprisoning a dead girl's body while it lay rotting in the heat."

Bristling, Smith leaned across the desk and pointed his finger at Maya. "We don't know nothing about no dead girl, and we don't have any Al Bard listed in our employees' records. Never heard of the guy. If he says we sent him to pick something up at the docks, he's a lyin' sack of shit."

"No, he isn't. I mean he *is* a lyin' sack of shit. You got that right. But he isn't mistaken about you employing him. He's working out a deal with his lawyer right now to tell us everything he knows about the little operation you have set up here—"

Interrupting, bristling like a cat with his tail clamped between the teeth of a pissed-off bulldog, he spat out the words, "You can talk to my lawyer, too."

Acting reasonable, Maya smiled, pure devilment turning up the sides of those pretty lips that Nik couldn't take his eyes off of. "Look, bud, if you want to tell me where I can find your father, I'd prefer to talk to the real boss, and not a snot-nosed kid whose daddy never trained him properly in dealing with the law."

Freaking out big-time, Smith lunged to his feet and pointed at the still open door where three, over-sized, stomach-protruding workers stood waiting. "Get out and don't come back without a warrant."

Nik, who'd automatically moved between the angry man and Maya, gave him a shove back in his chair. "Whoa, slow down, Junior, and listen to the lady."

Maya pulled out a card, passed it over. "You tell Smith Senior we want to see him. He's to come into the office within twenty-four hours or we'll send officers and a squad car to his home and have him picked up." Then she turned and headed for the doorway. Without any hesitation, she sauntered past the men who made way for her and only closed ranks on Nik, squeezing him enough that he itched to retaliate.

For a few seconds, the biggest dude, decaying teeth and breath smelling like he'd lunched on rotten fish, looked as if he'd push some buttons. Nik smiled and waited. A slap on the arm from one of the other fatsos convinced the sucker to back down, but only a few inches. And Nik didn't know if he was glad or not.

Thing was—the night Max took the beating—the only description he'd had to give was that one of his attacker's breath had been so disgusting that it had almost made him puke.

A fraternal protectiveness Nik had only ever felt for his soldiers raised its powerful head. Without conscious thought, he moved. His hand pushed the guy's chin so far upward, it came close to breaking bones. Knowing exactly how to place those hits so they didn't quite kill, Nik felt utmost satisfaction when he saw that the guy would be out of action for some time. Unfortunately, the others took umbrage at this treatment of their partner and moved in immediately. Grabbing an arm as the fist of one man came toward him; Nik used it as a lever to throw him at the other advancing man.

"Stop the bullshit! Unless you all want to be arrested for assaulting a Federal Agent, I suggest you boys calm down." Holding her gun in both hands, pointing it at Junior, Maya waited.

"Back off, boys. Just remember, Agent Barnes. Your man hit first. We could lay charges against him for police brutality."

"Not from where I stood. If Shithead hadn't tried blocking the way, Agent Foster wouldn't have had to convince him to move. Don't forget to tell your daddy what I said. He has twenty-four hours. And understand this: we'll have every exit in the city covered, so no unplanned trips."

Chapter 28

Once back in the car, Maya went for Nik. "What the hell were you thinking? They were hot for your blood. Didn't you see the way they acted when you followed me in there? Kinda like you were a zombie from 'The Return of the Living Dead.'" What she didn't share was that her stomach contents had all but emptied when she'd seen Nik retaliate and go for the biggest bruiser. Sweeping fear for her new partner registered a whole lot stronger than any worry for herself.

"Yeah, I got the feeling a few of them were shocked. But others weren't. Obviously, they already knew about Max's miraculous recovery."

"You think they were the drive-by shooters?"

"Don't know. Which reminds me, let's stop by my hotel room and see if Julian is still around. I have some questions to ask about the bar he says he danced in."

Maya swiftly floored the pedal and performed a noisy, squealing, U-turn, heading toward his place. She turned to Nik, who sat relaxed, the only telltale sign of irritation at the way she handled the car was that his dimple had gotten deeper.

Chuckling, she admitted, "After your friend disappeared from Nellie's, I tried having him brought in, but it's like the man's a ghost. No one can pick up his trail."

"Yeah, I know what you mean. He shadowed me at the beginning, couldn't shake the jerk. Then he disappeared. I told him he could stay in the room, so I'm hoping he's smart enough to hide out there. In case he was right and they were actually after him and not me, it's as good a place to lay low as any other."

Soon they were walking through the lobby, past the pool, and Nik had his key in the lock of the second door from the entrance. At once, Maya could see the room was empty. There were still belongings scattered around the place, but no sign of the man himself.

"He's not here." Nik was disappointed but didn't sound too surprised.

"Knowing him the way you do, where else would you look for him?"

"I don't know him."

She watched as Nik made a discovery that didn't seem to please him.

"The little shit found out a lot more about me than I ever did about him. Of course, he hacked into my computer to do it, but still…"

Maya added, "So you knew he'd poked around?"

"Yeah! I'm kind of weird about my property now that I have this cloud hanging over me from Max's situation. Just being extra careful."

"You're being smart. Gotta admit, though, I kind of liked the shmuck. I hope he's okay."

Nik grinned in agreement. Then put his hands on his hips and leaned back against the open doorway. "You feel like slumming tonight?"

Stunned and not hiding it, Maya replied, "Sure. Where and why?"

"The Pink Pussycat, to see if that's the joint where Julian might have danced."

"Ah, got you! You figure because Al Bard has a con-nection there with his girlfriend, it might be the very place where Juli rescued those girls. It's a long shot, but what the hell. We have nothing to lose."

Nik chuckled, his laugh lines playing havoc with his normally deadpan expression. "Never know. Stranger things have happened."

Maya had to stop herself from going over to the man and hauling his ass down on the king-size bed. God, with him around, reactions happened to her body that no one else had ever stimulated. Made her wet, hungry and annoyed for feeling that way.

Controlling her impulses, she changed the subject. "By the way, those freed girls all disappeared. As soon as I heard Juli's story, I had the uniforms out screening all known places where runaways or virtual strangers to America would normally end up. There's not a sign of any of them."

"And that's strange?"

"Of course! They'd need help with the language and money, places to stay. Poor misfits will have to find a way to get back home. Not much they can do living here, except to become a prostitutes or maids. Look, we'll go tonight; maybe some of the dancers will remember Juli and will know where we can hook up with him. It's a long shot, but as you said: stranger things have happened."

Chapter 29

Nik was floored. He couldn't believe how stunning Maya looked and how wonderful she smelled. In a body-hugging, silky dress, so low-cut her lush breasts all but escaped the gauzy green stuff covering them; she made all his senses kick into overdrive.

As he held the door open for her to go first, her spiked heels forced her ass to move in a way that had him clenching his fists to stop from sweeping her up, turning back into her place and trying his luck.

She'd done something to her hair; piled it on top of her head. Now her smooth, tanned neck lay bare, flaunting a come-on to starving lips. He licked his and stopped when he realized what he'd done.

Easy, tiger! Rein it in a little.

Not wanting to make small talk, he appreciated that Maya gave up after a few tries. She seemed to sense his reluctance, and, being a smart broad, settled back against the cooled leather seat of Max's Lexus CT and acted like a content passenger.

Earlier he'd had a hell of a time deciding what Max

would wear to a joint like this one. He knew what he'd choose. But his brother didn't dress like him at all. Trying to think like Max was a bummer. Finally he'd called him and asked.

"Hey, Nik, everything okay?"

"Yeah, sure."

"You didn't report back on what happened today. Bro, I want in on everything."

"The day's not over yet. I'll talk to you later. For now, I need to know what you'd wear to a joint like the Pink Pussycat?"

"The Pink Pussycat's a dive. First of all, I'd never go to a joint like that." Max's disgust could be plainly heard and made Nik laugh. "And second, if I'm in there undercover, I wouldn't dress like me, right? Therefore, you choose what makes you comfortable. And call me! I'm going crazy here."

"Right. Later."

Nik felt better knowing he could use his own duds and dress according to how he liked to look. Rather than styling his hair like Max, he wore it combed to the side so the wave dropped over his forehead. And he'd put away the fancy ring and watch. If Maya didn't like him wearing the short-sleeved, black and bright blue cotton plaid shirt and hipster jeans, well that was just too bad.

***

Finding a parking place around the back of the joint, he made out the stairway in the dark and his heartbeats revved. *Ah!* Julian's description fit. A doorway just underneath those stairs led to the basement.

Before he could discuss his find with Maya, a voice called out from the near the side of the building. "Hey, man, the parking's on the right. This here is private." Nik waved, started the car to turn it around and spotted a fancy bus pulling in, painted on the side with the performer's name: *The Misfits*. He knew these guys from years ago.

"Maya, I think I know of a way to get us in there with no hassles. Look, the band comes from around where I grew up. I used to know them. I'm going over to see how many of them remember me, see if we can tag along as part of their group so we don't stick out."

Surprise lit her expression, but she didn't question his decision, rather she nodded. "Good idea."

Chapter 30

Maya, waiting in the car for Nik to return, wiped her hands on a hanky and used it to remove the damp sheen from her chest. From the minute Nik had shown up at her door, she knew they had a...a party they needed to plan. An intimate twosome so they could take their attraction to the next level.

Her libido, sick of the starvation diet she'd followed for far too long, was actively bouncing back every time she laid eyes on Nik. When he showed up tonight wearing his sex-provoking outfit—filling those jeans snugly and the shirt that made his muscles obvious and his eyes glow deeper—*whoa!* It was all she could do to keep her knees from buckling, her hands to herself and her instinct to whimper under control.

Overreacting to the man, she'd had the urge to beg him to delay their evening's arrangements, remain at her house and make out. They could try it over and over again—just to get it right. Itching to get her hands on his sleek body, she acknowledged it *would* happen.

The shirt he'd chosen transformed his eyes from just

blue to "oh-my-God-your-eyes-are-gorgeous" blue. And his jeans fit him perfectly, sculpting his maleness, enticing her like a dog in heat.

Recognizing the flare of passion that he hadn't been able to hide quickly enough, she'd forced herself to look away from his aroused, narrow-eyed gaze and clamp her lips to stop them from begging.Knowing how much he wanted her too just made the inevitable so much sweeter.

***

In a short time, she was moving along with the three man, one woman band, pretending they were all part of the same group. Just before they entered the darkened, sleazy, yet full bar, Nik had introduced them. He'd been right in thinking they were the same people he'd known from his younger years.

The table they were given was right up against the stage where their previously set-up instruments rested: two guitars, a keyboard, a violin, and drums.

A waitress, who turned out to be Al Bard's hottie, Sadie Moore, sidled up to the band leader, Bob. After getting his order, leaning over unnecessarily, she made sure the other men got a good look down the front of her off-the-shoulder outfit while she wrote down their drink orders. Paying scant attention to the two women, she wiggled her way over to the next table full of drunks and idiots, all male.

Gail, the female drummer, clung onto Nik and was beginning to piss Maya off with her possessive attitude. "Nikky, baby, hell and tarnation, I've missed you, sugar! Why didn't you ever return?"

"Years pass quickly, Gail. Too much happening."

Looking downhearted, Gail rubbed her head against Nik's shoulder and groaned. "I know what you mean, honey. I surely do."

Finally, the boys got ready to start the first set and Gail reluctantly followed. Nik broke away from the clinger and came to sit near Maya. The other three band members seemed like nice guys, glad to meet up with a bud and more than happy to have him and her sit at their table. She liked them.

Soon they began to play and the western rhythm of their music shocked her. She'd expected a rock band at the very least. Funny thing was, the crowd loved the sound and pretty soon they were on their feet, two-stepping and having a good ol' time.

Nik held his hand out to her and she gladly stood up, moved into his waiting arms and began swinging to the beat. She loved the way his body cradled hers, wrapping her up in such a manner that she felt protected from other enthusiastic dancers.

He smiled down at her, the dimple sweetly appearing—making her heart seize for a few seconds. "Did I tell you how nice you look? Green suits you. And I like what you did to your hair."

Not used to a man paying compliments that weren't wrapped up in fancy words, but were plain and heartfelt, she gave back in the same way. "Thanks, *sugar*. Black and blue looks good on you too." Unfortunately, her choice of words was questionable.

His smile started to fade, probably not sure if she was playing him or not. "Seriously, Nik, the shirt does wonders for those eyes you like to flash around." *Shit, she just couldn't seem to stop teasing.*

This time he laughed, winked and gave her the full benefit of the havoc those very eyes could create. Then, over her head, he gazed around the room and stopped when his sparklers landed on Sadie. "We need to talk to the waitress, see if she remembers Julian."

"You mean *you* need to talk to her. She won't have anything to do with the likes of me. I'm missing one very important body part that just might get her to cooperate."

Grinning, visibly delighted with her dry response, Nik swung her past the rowdy dancers crowding them, using it as an excuse to mold her tightly against his hardened body.

As soon as she noticed his condition, not only did she rub herself against the protrusion, she looked him in the eye, invitation plain. She wanted him, too.

***

That did it! He licked her neck, couldn't stop the action, didn't want to. Her moan of pleasure spurred him on to taking even more liberties. With his chest glued to hers, their lower halves moving together as if joined, he kissed the soft skin under her ears and along the slope of her sweetly perfumed shoulder. Loving that her arms lifted to curl around his neck, their bodies now as close as possible, he lost himself in her taste and the smell of her arousal.

Intimately, hot and heavy, their breathing quickened. Abandoning control, his hands moved from her waist to travel lower, gliding along the silken protrusion of the sweetest ass he'd...

"Hey, guys and gals, can you all give a big welcome to Nik Baudin. Let's get him up here on the stage to sing his rendition of an old Clint Black favorite—*Killing Time*. This man can really make sweet music, so put your hands together and show him some love." Gail's voice rang out with false heartiness.

His name being called over the mic instantly brought Nik back to his senses. Between the catcalls, whistles, and foot-stomping, he had no choice but to lead a puzzled, unhappy Maya back to their table and head up the stairs. Once on stage, he took the guitar that Bob held out, and his dazzling grin, along with the first strum on the instrument, quieted the rowdiness. Waiting to see if they would love him or boo, the silence built.

Chapter 31

Maya couldn't believe the raspy velvet tones of pure country that settled the crowd in an instant to slavish adoration. In no time at all, the dancers were back on the floor, passing the stage with their thumbs up and smiles of pure pleasure. *This make-believe cowboy of hers could sing.*

She couldn't take her eyes off the big man who hugged his guitar, playing it with the ease of a seasoned entertainer. Not too comfortable revealing her wide-eyed adoration, she stared down at her clasped hands, clamping down on the titillation that raised her already overheated enthusiasm to catastrophic levels.

While Nik flaunted his talent, playing to the crowd, a bolt of shock hit her hard, making her reel. She knew nothing about this man she so badly wanted in her bed. He was virtually a stranger even though he seemed familiar because of his likeness to her partner.

So why had Nik appeared in the picture now that Max was gone? She needed to know more. Like where he came from? And what he was really doing in New Orleans? Was he truly with the Special Forces, and if so, why wasn't he on duty?

Her stomach roiled in anxiety and triggered a headache. As much as she hated to admit her blunder in turning a blind eye, it was past time for the rose-colored-glasses to be taken off while she dug out the truth. What was she thinking? What had happened to her need-to-know-everything gene?

As Charlie used to say, *hell and damnation!* She was an FBI agent with a whole lot of talented people and equipment at her disposal. If requested, they could find out anything she wanted to know within a few minutes of digging.

Except... that might well throw up some red flags. People could ask why she wanted this particular info. It would tie the two brothers together, even though their last names weren't the same. Uncover Nik's true identity and her part in the switch. Best she hold off on an official search and just ask the man himself.

The crowd's shouting caught her attention and she realized they didn't want Nik to stop. They were screaming for more.

Waiting to see if they would talk him into another song, she glanced around the room and spotted Sadie looking enthralled. Ah! If Nik played her right, he might get something from his adoring admirer. As though he knew what was going through Maya's mind, he began promising to perform the rendition of a song she'd never heard before. Not a fan of country, *until now*, her lack of knowledge about the music hadn't been an issue.

"If ya' all settle down, I'll sing one more song for you lovers out there. It's a favorite of mine by Johnny Reid."

Suddenly, the chorus line of his next tune caught her attention. "A Woman Like You" had every hot-blooded female wriggling in her seat and wiping the heat from her flushed face. The fact that he sent his dimpled smiles Maya's way during most of the song gave her incredible pleasure. *Oh, baby! Screw the questions. We're going to party tonight!*

Calling for a break after the tune ended to boot-stomping admiration, the band left the stage. Handshakes and back pats for Nik were shared before they split in different directions, some moving to the bar and others out back for a cigarette. Gail aimed for the table where Nik was headed. When she saw Maya stand and gesture to the back door, she shrugged, scooped her purse from the side of the table and turned in the direction of the restroom.

Taking him by the hand, Maya stopped and looked at him from under her lashes. "We need to talk."

"About?"

"You. I just realized I know next to nothing about you."

"What do you want to know? That I have the hots for you so badly, I can't think of anything else but getting you home and undressed." His smile dazzled her and almost made her forget the reason she'd pulled him away from the others.

"Hold that thought. First we talk and then... " She pulled her eyes from his knowing gaze and nodded her head toward the bar. "Sadie is smitten with you. Her eyes almost popped out of her head when you were singing. A little schmoozing and you might be able to get some information. You up for it?"

"Are you kidding? Another play on words?"

The fact that he looked uncomfortable, even crabby, about performing went a long way to settling her upset stomach and pounding temples. She laughed and shook her head. "Wasn't thinking. Sorry."

He shook his head, his dimple clearly visible. "Yeah!

Whatever! If it finds us Julian, I guess it'll be worth it."

Maya watched as he sauntered over to the end of the bar where Sadie waited for a tray of drinks the bartender was preparing. When the woman saw him approach, she beamed a welcome and sidled closer. Nik wrapped his arm around her shoulder and began talking in her ear.

Not wanting to be caught glaring and staring, Maya headed for the lady's room to see if she could pump Gail. Sounded like her and Nik went back years. Hell, anything she could learn about the guy would help her understand what drove him and why he would put himself in the dangerous position he'd taken on.

Chapter 32

Sitting in the car in front of Maya's house, Nik finally broke the silence. "Maya, you haven't said two words all the way home. I'm really sorry I couldn't get more out of Sadie. She knew Julian Freed, said he'd danced there a few times, not as an entertainer in the way he'd led us to believe, but as a customer. He'd befriended the bar girls and paid for a lot of free drinks. Since I'd described him as gay, she wasn't even sure it was the same person. She only knew him as a regular guy who called himself Julian, not Juli."

"It's not that. I'm under no illusions that you got all that you could from her. I guess I'm still trying to digest what Gail had to say about *you*."

"Why am I not surprised? I saw you follow her to the ladies' room. Wondered if you'd question her? You do have a way."

"It's my job. Except, she was more forthcoming than most of the perps I have to interrogate. Darn woman wouldn't stop talking about you. She told me about you as a teenager, how you'd hooked up with them, sneaking into the bars as an adult and supported yourself through college before disappearing."

"Yeah, so?"

"She said you were pretty wild."

"I was."

"Mentioned that your father had been a mean bastard and came to drag you out of the joints they played in sometimes. That you never stopped him."

"That happened when I was still fifteen. He was a big man. Not much I could do." Nik's voice had hardened and he looked away from her, the smile long gone.

"Then you left, never said a word. Just disappeared."

"Uh, huh."

"Didn't you ever retaliate? Get your own back?"

"Not till I was sixteen. Scared the shit out of me so badly that I left. As a kid, I was always terrified that I might have inherited his mean streak. That if I ever started with him, I might not be able to stop. Hell, the only way I could make sure it never surfaced again was to learn control. The Navy taught me that and a hell of a lot more."

"Nellie told me why didn't you grow up with her and Max. About how they left you behind when they moved to New Orleans. It must have devastated you to learn about a family you never knew existed

"It did, until I accepted that the total blame belonged to my ol' man, the cagey prick who wanted someone around to fetch and carry for him. I can't understand any other reason he'd keep me."

"Maybe as a way to pay back your mom for leaving."

"Could be. Wouldn't put it past him. You know, as a youngster, I'd have weird feelings of being abandoned, but they never made sense. I put them down to missing a dead mother and stopped letting them get to me years ago."

"Dead? Your father told you Nellie had died?"

"Yeah! They left when I was a two-year-old child and I believed everything he said...had no reason not to. All I cared about in those days was getting as far away from the Bastard as I could."

"Is he still alive?"

"No. Why?"

"Cause I wanted to find him and shoot the son-of-a-bitch."

Nik's laughter surprised them both. He slid his hand along her shoulder and squeezed gently "Look, don't feel sorry for me. I did odd jobs; some singing here and there, got to college and finally joined the armed forces. I found a family there."

"That's sad, Nik."

"It is what it is. I don't like thinking about this other stuff. I'm gonna scram. I'll see you tomorrow."

Nik knew he was being harsh, but he hated talking about his past. Every time he thought about the pigpen he'd called home, the drunken abuse, and the torment of living alone with a deranged scumbag, the bile in his stomach swirled.

A headache loomed, promising retribution. Clenching his muscles to stop from reaching for her, using her body to assuage the pain in his soul, he fought off the anger, but the rotten mood wouldn't leave. *Enough!* Time for him to head home, take his medication and hope that tonight he'd be able to sleep.

After seeing her to the door, delivering a peck on the cheek as thanks for putting up with his grumpiness, he pulled away from her driveway and headed in the direction of Max's apartment.

He noticed a flashy black car catch up to him too darn

fast as he traveled along Rampart Street, crowding him, the headlights appearing closer than any idiot's should be. Shit, if he stepped on the brakes, the other vehicle would crawl right up his ass.

Fuck!

The car drove into his back end, making him swerve and have to fight for control. Not a stunt driver like Maya, nevertheless, he could handle any four-wheeled vehicle easily. He floored the gas. So did the tailgater. Only it wasn't happy to stay behind him, it tried to pull up alongside.

Not gonna happen, asshole! Nik veered into its lane and then s-turned, taking up both. The move was one he hadn't tried since the days when he was a randy youth high on pot and life. Silently thanking Max for loving big engines, he figured his controlled U-turn would make any movie director clap his hands like a two-year-old.

Fighting to control the car, he floored it again and checked the side mirror. With the street almost empty, they had also managed to turn and were following again, just not so close.

A memory of a day wandering the city intruded. He remembered a side street he'd found nearby where the back lane wasn't noticeable unless one knew about it. Hoping his followers would pass on by, he spun around the corner, zigzagging through the streets until he came close to the turnoff. Flipping off his lights, he pulled into the lane by intuition and God's mercy. Once they flew past, he left his lights off and backed out, turning in the direction he'd come.

Continually glancing in his rear-view mirror, he realized he'd lost them for now. But, they were on to him, or at least Max's car. Probably wasn't a good idea to hang out at his brother's apartment tonight either. Instead, he drove in the direction of his hotel where he could leave the car behind an empty house a few blocks away and walk to his destination.

An hour later, he was still pacing his room. Since there wasn't much to report, calling Max on the burner phone they'd set up took no time at all. He didn't mention the car chase. Why rile up his twin who was paranoid enough about this undercover role? Nor did he have much to share in the way of their case, or news about the Mosleys. He did notice budding excitement on Max's part when he described the Smith & Sons operation. Max insisted, in fact made Nik promise, that he'd report everything the old man said if he appeared at the office the next day for questioning.

"Keep your eyes open, bro. Those guys play for keeps."

"Gotcha! Got to sleep now. I'll call you again tomorrow. Oh, yeah, tell Linda thanks for not blowing it today when Maya and I appeared at the restaurant. Turns out, Maya loves the po' boys in there."

"I know. Who do you think introduced her to them? Night dude. Be careful."

Nik grabbed water from the mini-fridge and took another cold, three-minute shower. Every time he thought about his sexy partner in that green dress, he called himself all kinds of names. *How could you walk away from those needy arms, man? She wanted you. You're one dumb shit!*

Lying naked on top of the white comforter, he thought about the evening. It was the first time he'd ever dedicated a particular song to anyone. At first, it felt kind of cheesy. But once he'd listened to the words that Johnny Reid had made famous, he knew they suited his growing attraction for Maya. *It had felt like heaven when she'd wrapped her arms around him.*

Shit! He slammed his hand down on the night table and reached for his phone. Trepidation rode him hard, almost made him give up after the second ring until he heard her husky, welcoming voice and his whole body reacted.

Smiles changed his face from grim to pleased. Lightness filled his soul—and the opposite engorged his body.

Chapter 33

Maya reached for the phone, her hand shaking when she saw Max's number. "Nik! You called." Could he hear her excitement, her pleasure? She hadn't tried to hide it.

"You told me to. Said we could keep each other company when we couldn't sleep. Did I wake you?"

"Kind of."

"Kind of?"

Maya giggled, amused by the instant worry in his tone. "Okay, not really! My body isn't settling down like it should. Seems to think it missed out on something exceptional tonight."

"Mine too. Damn shame."

"You can say that again. I hope you know it was you who blew it."

"I do know. And I can't tell you how much I'm mourning my stupidity. We *were* going to make out tonight, weren't we?"

Maya knew her chuckle sounded regretful, but she was damned if she could help herself. The guy tickled her into acting silly. "I like a man who comes straight to the point."

"Quit hedging. You didn't answer my question. We were, weren't we?"

"Sure looked that way, cowboy."

"You liked my song?"

"Which one?"

"'A Woman Like You.' The second one."

"Bet you sang that to a lot of girls before." Maya held her breath for his answer. Dammit...it mattered too much!

"Nope! Didn't even know it existed in the days I played the honky-tonks. But the moment I heard it, I knew I had to sing it to... to someone special one day."

Was that hesitation she'd heard? Okay, those words, spoken in the rough tones of a sincere man, were starting to unravel the thick rope she'd tied her heart up with years ago. *Merde*, this surprisingly sensitive guy was getting to her. The silence dragged on while she thought of how to answer without giving away too much trust. Yet at the same time, being careful she didn't make him feel like he'd overstepped. *Fuck! I'm no good at this romance stuff.*

"Maya?" Damn straight there was uncertainty. She sensed him backing away and knew she'd have to share fast if she wanted to save the moment. "Yeah, Nik. I really liked the song. Made me want to stand up so that everyone in the place knew you were singing it for me." *Did I go too far? Shit, shit... shit. I stink at this lovey-dovey talk.*

He groaned, and she knew it was a good sound. He liked what she'd said. That came through the line clearly. She breathed a sigh of relief.

"I want you! Dammit, woman, I should be there with you now... "

He broke off his word with a faint exclamation and she heard a rustling movement. "What, Nik? What's going on?"

His whisper could barely be heard. "Someone's paying a visit. I'm fine. Don't worry." When he ended the call, the click sounded like a loud bang.

Instant fear shot straight to her adrenal glands, charging them like a detonator on a bomb. The sickening rush that followed effectively shook her to the core, making it impossible to think straight. Something she prided herself on—not getting rattled—wasn't working for her now. She ignored the churning in her stomach and tried to think. Her fists pressed hard against her mouth, stopping the building sobs from escaping.

Get dressed!

Rushing around, gathering discarded work clothes from the chair where she'd left them, she dressed and flew out the door in less time than it took to call for backup.

They'd get to Max's place first. She was further away but then she drove faster. Not one to pray—she didn't believe prayers made a difference. They hadn't when she'd lost Charlie.

Therefore shock hit hard when she heard herself repeating "Please, God!" over and over... But she didn't stop.

Chapter 34

Nik was glad he'd turned the lights out before calling Maya. The darkness now gave him an advantage. When he heard the lock ping and saw the handle slowly turning, he was already crouched in place behind the door.

Waiting for the culprit to show himself, he slowed his heartbeat and assumed the cold persona of a black ops pro. Whoever decided to break into his place tonight would be sorry. He sure as hell wasn't in the mood to play games. *No mercy!*

First he heard murmurs, and then the door began to swing in. It stopped. Clothes rustling came next. Heavy breathing followed as if someone had laid something down.

Damn good thing Julian hit the lights before he'd stepped fully inside or his recovery would have been in a hospital bed.

Furious, Nik growled like a wolf whose prey had escaped. Then he let go of the smaller man with a shove to emphasize his temper. "What the hell are you doing breaking into the room at this time of the night?" He stalked over to the desk to replace his gun and picked up his pants.

Acting weird, Julian motioned to someone before stepping further into the room and closing the door. "No need to dress on my account."

"Stop pissing me off any more than you already have. I could have killed you. Don't you know it's dangerous sneaking around—"

"Hey! I wasn't sneaking around. I just came to drop off some clothes and get something out of the safe. You did tell me I could use the place, remember?"

Feeling rather sheepish at his uncalled-for anger, Nik nodded. "Yeah. Sorry." Pissed that he'd been so jumpy and had broken off his phone call for nothing, it took him awhile to cool down.

Julian stepped past him. "What are you doing here anyway? I thought you were playing your twin's special agent role? Staying at his place."

"How did you know that? I didn't tell anyone." Nik stomped over to Julian with the full intention of making him talk. But he stopped when the little guy didn't even flinch. His expression of calm cheerfulness never wavered. "Christ, you piss me off."

"Why? Because I know what you're up to? I told you, I'm your shadow. You might not see me, but it doesn't mean I'm not around."

Nik couldn't fathom that this dude was as skillful as his words led one to believe. Shaking his head, he went to grab the water bottle and drank it dry. "Who's that with you?"

"No one." Julian's expression finally changed, went serious and then crafty. "You're hearing things, sugar."

"Stop working me. And I don't hear *things*. I'm trained to listen and I know what went on. There was someone with you. You can deny it all you want, but I know what I heard."

Julian headed to the closet and knelt down by the safe. His muffled words were low but clear to Nik. "Man! A guy can't even have a rendezvous without getting grilled like a punk teenager. I'm outta here." Slipping a wad of money into his pocket, he closed the safe and reset the combination. "Go back to sleep, Nik, and see if next time you can't wake up on the right side of the bed."

"Hey, I want to ask you some questions. You have some explaining to do."

Still indignant, Julian waved at Nik as if to say later, and walked on past as if he wasn't even there. Before Nik could react to what was going down, the door closed behind the pest. Lunging forward, Nik swung it open in time to see a smaller person's shadow step out from behind the bougainvillea, join Julian, and they both faded into the darkness.

Chapter 35

Nik quickly returned to his phone and tried to call Maya back. She didn't answer even after he let it ring numerous times. Not pleased with the lack of connection, he threw himself on the bed and decided he'd wait for ten minutes and then try again.

His glance fell on the safe in the closet and he went over to it. Kneeling down, he tried all kinds of combinations, hoping he'd luck out and hit on the right one, but of course it didn't happen.

Suddenly a knock sounded and he heard a familiar voice call his name. Moving swiftly, he swung the door open just as Maya had lined up to kick it in. Before he knew what hit him, her foot struck his stomach, landing in his solar plexus. Since he'd guessed who was at the door, he hadn't readied his muscles to take a hit and the shock almost floored him.

"What the hell!" Doubled over, he tried to catch his breath.

"Nik!" Maya lowered her gun and swept her gaze around the room behind him. "You're okay..."

Feeling the pain ebb, he couldn't help the glad smile when he saw the relief flood her face. Probably wasn't a smart idea to goad a woman so close to hysterics.

Catching enough breath to be stupid, and with not enough brain proficiency to stop himself, he croaked, "I was until you showed up."

"How the hell can you tease when I was sure they'd gotten to you?" Furious, anxiety riding her hard, she swung her arm toward his face, intending to plow her fist into his grin.

Of course, he stopped her. Gently, carefully, he gathered her into his arms so she couldn't gouge his eyes out next. Finally, she slumped and let her head fall onto his chest.

"You jackass, why didn't you call me back? I was frantic. When you hung up, I thought you'd called from Max's apartment. I went there and had the uniforms follow me." She shivered.

"Darlin', I did call you. You never answered." Cuddling her body, he gathered her still closer, wrapping his arms around her, taking care to gently imprison her just in case she erupted again. He lowered his cheek to rest on the top of her head and got off on the protective feeling that washed over him.

Her voice broke into his dreamy state. "It's a hell of a mess!"

"What's a hell of a mess? Are you talking about Max's place?"

"Uh-huh. Someone broke in and trashed the joint. Ruined most of his clothes, smashed his TV. Shit, everything was... you know."

Sad for his brother, Nik wished he'd been there to stop them. If he could have caught the trasher, maybe they'd have a clue as to who was behind the violence.

Approaching footsteps warned Nik that they had visitors. Instinctively, he guided Maya toward the back of the door. Positioning himself in front, he snatched Max's gun from the desk.

Maya's hand over his stopped him from further action. "Chill! It's my backup."

Sure enough, Henry Lassiter stepped gingerly into the room, his gun held in both hands by his side. When he saw Nik and Maya, both unharmed, he holstered his weapon and waved off the group following behind him. Turning to face Nik, his expression revealed that of a disgruntled friend. "Hey, Foster. Sounds like you've been having a lot of fun tonight." He spoke with a distinct grouchiness of a person in a snit. "Wanna tell me why you stood me up earlier? And... why you're staying in a hotel room instead of your apartment?"

Maya slid her hands in the back pockets of her pants and looked away, her body language clearly indicating she'd leave it up to him to answer the question.

"Yeah, well. I have a friend visiting from out of town. We had a few drinks and I decided to crash here for the night."

"Probably a good idea. So where's your friend now?"

Before Nik could form another lie, Julian walked in through the still partially opened door, waving a pizza. "Got it, man. They were still open. Hi, Maya. Sugar, you look delicious—as always."

Chapter 36

Frustration and lack of sleep kept Nik from being a happy camper. "Where the hell did you disappear to?"

Julian pointed to himself, pretending shock. "Why are you so pissed off with me? I just went to get us a pizza."

Nik could smell the lie as much as he could smell the savory cheese and mushrooms. He couldn't force Julian into being truthful if he didn't intend to be, but he sure as hell didn't like being played.

Losing patience while being interrogated by Lassiter, and then adding frustration as Maya left with him, Nik picked Julian up by the front of his shirt and let him dangle on the tips of his toes. Pushing his face within an inch of the other man's, he let loose. "I want it all, what your business is here in New Orleans. How you know me and my brother. And why you keep showing up at the most opportune times."

"Sorry, dude, I can't tell you. Either you have to kill me, which you'd never do, or hurt me, which I'm a bit worried you'd enjoy. Or share a piece of that mouth-watering pizza with me before I starve to death."

***

After gorging on three pieces, Nik wiped his mouth on the napkin and shook his head at the offer of the last slice. "Nope. I'm stuffed. Look, can you at least tell me if the joint where you mentioned finding the trafficked girls was called the Pink Pussycat?"

"As a matter of fact."

"Quit playing games. Does that mean yes or no?"

"Yes. But I don't think they're using that place to stash the girls anymore. And before you try grilling me for their new location, I don't have it."

"Do you know where the girls disappeared to? The ones you released?"

"Some of them."

"Will you just tell me?" Feeling slightly less irritated, Nik played the game with Julian, whose grin hinted at the enjoyment he felt from their banter.

"Soon. I just need to clear it with the boss."

Interested in learning that Julian wasn't working alone, Nik played along. "And I suppose you won't tell me your boss's name."

"Gotta clear that also."

"This boss must be some guy to earn your loyalty like this. I'd sure like to meet him."

"Oh, man, you already have." Julian laughed and moved over to his couch at the back of the room. "I'm bushed. See you in the morning."

Exasperated, Nik decided Julian had won that battle. Hopefully, the next day, Smith Senior might be more forthcoming. He couldn't wait to grill the lowlife in the FBI interview room.

Chapter 37

Armed with the questions Max had fed him, Nik didn't take into consideration the expertise of a smarmy lawyer who was paid big bucks to keep criminals out of jail. And Smith had hired the chief dick of the slime pool.

The two danced around every question he or Maya asked, joking, acting cool and untroubled. "Your son told us that Al Bard wasn't on your payroll. Mr. Smith, do you really expect me to believe that this man stole one of your trucks, then broke into your office and made himself out a pick-up order, so he could then go to the port and procure an empty container? Come on..." Maya's repulsed expression spoke louder than words.

"That stupid kid is my step-son. And he takes after his real father—a loser. My wife insisted that he should work in the office."

"And you mind your wife. What does that make you?" Maya shared a grin with Nik. "What's the term they use nowadays?"

Nik replied, disgust overriding self-control. "I'd call it being pussy- whipped."

Ignoring their byplay, the two posers put their heads together and the whispering started up again. Nik wanted to hit something—preferably one, or both, of the idiots at the table. Watching Maya closely, he didn't know how she maintained such a cool façade. Then she glanced his way and he saw the simmering anger buried under layers of professionalism, and his respect for her skills soared.

Smith, an exceedingly unlikeable man, cloaked in bravado and a flashy white suit, played with his skinny mustache continuously. Finally he nodded in agreement and answered Maya's question about Al. "Turns out my wife's son had it wrong. The man does work for us on a temporary basis, only *we* know him as Birdy Bard. And he was sent to get that container, which was supposed to be empty. But we don't know nothing else about the terrible situation with any dead girl."

"You mean to tell me that you weren't aware of her escaping from your men who picked up a delivery at that very terminal four nights ago? Hard to believe! You do remember that your crew was there to collect a shipment of electrical machinery? And we believe that hidden in that cargo was a smaller container imprisoning the young female hostages shipped to you from Singapore."

Smith sat with a dumb smirk on his face, a twitching eyelid and sweat beginning to pool on his neck. Pretending to be unaffected, he pursed his lips and said nothing.

Nik stuck his hands in his pockets. Forced to control the urge to wipe the stupidness off Smith's ugly mug, he had to do something. With an eyebrow raised, Maya shot him a warning, which came through loud and clear.

Ultimately, the lawyer spoke up. "Mr. Smith runs a very lucrative shipping company. Of course he has freight arriving from Singapore. That's where his family has a factory that produces electrical machinery."

"Yes, we know. Lee Electrical is a very small company and yet it's surprisingly prosperous." Maya flipped through some papers clipped to one side of a file folder.

"No law against that, Agent Barnes."

Maya nodded and turned to Smith. "Your brother runs the factory—is that right? The younger one called Lee Smith?"

"So?"

"And your first name is Maurice, is it not? No, don't bother checking with your lawyer. We have your files here and it states it quite plainly."

"I wasn't trying to hide my name, missy." Smith spat out the words, ignoring the earlier controversial subjects that Maya had introduced.

Nik interrupted. "Agent Barnes is her name, not missy. And answer the previous questions. Did the shipment of electrical machinery your brother Lee dispatched also include a hidden container of young girls?"

The lawyer stood and brushed his hands together. "This interrogation has a strong stench of harassment. Unless you have enough proof to charge my client, then I suggest you back off and we'll be on our way."

Knowing that they had gotten as far as they would get with the inquiry about the shipments, Maya changed tack. "One last question, if I may?" She blocked their escape route. Her piercing stare never wavered. "I'm thinking that the Mosley gang, which has shown up on the NOPD's radar a lot lately, could be made up from a composite of two names and not just be one person. Moe, short for Maurice, and Lee would fit the bill perfectly, don't you think, Mr. Smith? It is true that your friends call you Moe?"

Chapter 38

Maya watched Nik throughout the interview with Smith and she felt his disgust and frustration. Not being a real Fed, and without the experience of having interviewed numerous scumbags over the years, he didn't have the same restraint as that of a specialist.

After she'd scanned the files that had come through earlier about Lee Smith and extent of their business he ran in Singapore, it was pretty easy to piece the puzzle together. What pissed her off was that the Mosleys didn't even try to bury their involvement. In fact, Moe was down-right blasé. Which meant, they were satisfied there'd be no leaks about their operations that could be used by the police.

Knowing this, Maya didn't feel quite as positive about being able to uncover their setup. Sometimes it took months of hard work, scrutiny and numerous people to work such a case, and even then there were no guarantees they'd be able to make any arrests—unless they caught them red-handed.

Shit! Irritation gnawed at her faith, leaving her unsure.

What was the next step? To talk to Julian Freed in person and not just have his information come through Nik came to mind. There were a lot of questions she wanted answered. And he might be able to satisfy some of her curiosity.

Thinking of questions, she still hadn't found out what had happened to Max. And, as her partner, whether presumed dead or not, he deserved some of her attention.

Strangely, Nik didn't seem to be as near as concerned about his disappearance as she was. It could be because the brothers had only just met. Or maybe he knew something she didn't. Feeling unbalanced, she decided to play on her instincts and keep her eyes open—watch everyone—starting with Smith's operation. She needed to get some idea of what was happening in that office.

A meeting with her boss, Ron Bitters, as dicey as it was, got her what she wanted. He'd dispatch a surveillance team to observe the comings and goings from the run-down Smith & Sons office complex. Hoping that eventually something would appear out of place, she visualized an imminent warrant and a search of the premises.

She knew it was unlikely that they'd be holding any of the kidnapped girls there. But in the same way as when a peeping tom spied on folks nightly, every so often he'd get an eyeful. If they kept their attention on this operation, just maybe, they'd catch the gang breaking the law.

Chapter 39

"What do you mean you have no idea where to find Juli? I thought we'd decided the last time he disappeared that you needed to keep better track of him." Still smarting from her superior's tongue-lashing about there being no progress on the case, Maya got up from where she'd perched on the edge of her cluttered desk and stomped to the window.

Nik caught the full basket she'd dislodged just in time before the stack of papers hit the floor and scattered. "Hey, you don't understand. One minute he's there and the next he's gone."

"Yeah, I know someone else just like him." Her glare spoke the words she'd left out. "Look, do you at least have a phone number?"

"No. But I can leave him a message at the room. I know he's staying there and would eventually get it."

"Okay. Let's go. And then we'll stop at the Pink Pussycat and ask a few questions. I know they won't be very forthcoming there, but if we rattle the cage a little, who knows what kind of vermin we might shake up?"

Since the nightclub was closer, they parked in the empty lot and made their way to the front entrance. The show didn't start for a few hours so there wasn't much action at all. Seeing as how the front door stood open for a beer delivery, Maya boldly stepped into the dim interior and waited until her eyes became adjusted.

The stench of cigarette smoke from years past, stale beer and the soiled carpet got to Maya, and without all the lights on and the mob of booze-happy people, the place looked rather scummy and sad.

Having done her research, Maya knew the club had changed hands just recently. It was now owned by a multi-national company with a murky background they were still digging into. This holding company called M&L—which by itself rang bells— had recently bought up a lot of properties in New Orleans, and this particular nightclub was managed by Glen Lister.

Maya sauntered ahead with Nik following. She sensed his body behind her like a shield. It felt kind of good knowing the man had her back. Stopping a paunchy delivery fellow, his thin, gray, straggly beard hanging a foot down from his face, she said politely, "I'm Agent Barnes, and this is my partner, Agent Foster." Maya moved her jacket so the man could see her badge. He leaned close as if his eyes were bad, but he'd gotten into her personal space and no one did that without paying. Before Nik could interfere, which she knew he wanted to do from the hiss she'd just heard, she lifted her arm, belting the idiot on the chin enough to throw his head back. "Oops! Sorry. Look, do you know where I can find the manager?"

Sheepishly, he backed up, rubbed his chin and swore under his breath. "Yeah! He's probably the asshole in the back office, yelling at his secretary, just through that hallway." A beefy finger pointed her in the direction where cuss words, followed by a slap and a scream, could be heard.

Moving swiftly, Nik striding by her side, they entered the room together. A quick glance and she took in the situation. The secretary holding her cheek, tears pouring over her heavily made-up face, cowered in the corner, while a short, wiry prick in black slacks and a yellow golf shirt advanced on her threateningly.

"Back off, mister. You've had your fun." Maya threatened Lister with her badge obvious and her hand on her weapon.

Too stupid to know when the game was up, rage still riding him, Lister swung at her instead and ended up flying through the air. Nik had seen her warning hand motion to back off and she'd give him a gold star later for listening. This guy was hers and she fully intended to teach the scumbag a lesson.

His temper fueled with pain and embarrassment, the dickhead just didn't know when to stop. He rolled to his feet and lunged at her, intending to use his body like a battering-ram.

Oh, goody! I love this move... Using his bent knee as her stepping stool, she literally ran up his body flipped over and rammed her feet in his chest, then ended up in a crouch. Hearing Nik's laugh made her insides glow. Her various step-daddies sure did come in handy.

A short time later, Maya and Nik sat in chairs across from Lister, waiting for him to regain his senses. They had agreed to hear what the man had to say before setting anything in motion. After all, they had him over a lawbreaking barrel, and just maybe he'd be more forthcoming if he thought they might loosen up and make a deal.

Quitting her job, and now long-gone, the disgusted secretary didn't help them very much. She'd known nothing of any activities around the joint that might not be honest. And Maya believed her since she'd exhibited her utmost desire to get back at the bastard for messing up her face. That, plus the fact that she'd only been on the job for a few days, made her declaration reasonable.

Nik stood, paced from one end of the room to the other, his countenance indicating his unrest. "Sure is taking his time." They both glanced at the sad sucker propped up in his chair, head lolling to the side and saliva drooling from his slack mouth. "You must have put a lot more wallop into that incredible kick than it looked like from where I was standing."

"It is pretty effective."

"It's just damn pretty, period."

Not wanting to wait any longer, Nik went to the sink in the corner by the coffee area and came back with a carafe of cold water, which he threw into Lister's face. Sputtering, his red face dripping and registering shock, the coward cringed in his chair and looked first at Nik and then Maya. "What the hell do you want?"

Voice chirpy with glee totally fueled by satisfaction, Maya responded, "I'm Agent Barnes, the person you tried to assault a little while ago. And this is my partner, Agent Foster. We'd like to ask you a few questions."

Wiping the water from his face with a hand shaking from the reaction of being injured, Lister spoke, or maybe groused would be a better description for the way he answered. "I got nothing to say. You broke into my place and harassed me. I'm thinking to call the police."

Maya shook her head, an expression of *who-do-you-think-you're-talking-to?* in her grim smile. "Hey, how about this? We charge you with assault against Marion Glendale, your former secretary, who, by the way, deserves full wages *and* a six-week hardship bonus. Add to that, attacking a federal officer in the line of duty—"

Lister ran his wet fingers through his comb-over, smoothing the greasy mass to the side. "Fine. You're blackmailing me. What do you want?"

"Just a few answers."

"About what?" Lister, now sitting straight in his chair, although his hand still rubbed his stomach, listened carefully. His glance skipped from Maya to Nik and back to who he considered to be in charge. "I have nothing to hide. Ask away."

Nik slowly moved over to sit on the edge of the desk closer to Lister's chair and leaned over the man threateningly. He didn't say a word. Maya loved the clever maneuver and nodded toward him. *He's good...*

"I'd think before answering because I don't have a lot of patience right now. When I look at any degenerate who likes to hit women and then calls himself a man, I just want to throw up. You know? So don't try me. Tell me about the shipment of young girls that arrived here on July fourteenth. We know they were brought to the basement and then disappeared—"

"What the hell are you talking about?" Aggressive again, Lister tried to push past her, but Nik made sure that didn't happen. Thrusting the idiot back into his seat, he motioned for Maya to continue.

"You sure do like to interrupt, don't you? That's not only rude, but it's also damned annoying."

"Can you blame me? I don't know anything about a shipment of girls. And they sure as hell never came to my nightclub. Chrissakes, I don't even have the fucking keys to the basement." He added that last sentence as if that was the final vindication to his story.

What got to Maya was—the man was telling the truth.

Chapter 40

Nik knew he'd done right by standing down and letting Maya take on Lister, but it ranked up there as one of the hardest things he'd ever had to do. As if she knew he'd step in, her waving him down before he could leap had stopped his forward momentum and left him with his heart in his throat, choking the spit right out of him. When she'd handled the asshole with all the aplomb of a veteran warrior and proved her ability to take care of herself, he'd had only one thought in his rattled head.

Thank-you-Lord!

It wasn't as if he hadn't known plenty of women in the forces who could take care of trouble just as well as any male, but in those situations, he'd never had his heart tied up in their welfare—not like he felt when he thought of Maya in danger. With no time to delve into his predicament right now, he instead faked being a relaxed partner. Meanwhile, his insides were being ripped into shreds from the shock and the recurring trauma symptoms from his PTSD.

He covered it up well, he thought. Hunching over an

agitated Lister helped him grip onto his control. Playing the bad cop to Maya's opposite role also calmed him enough that he was pretty sure she'd missed his reactions. One thing he did notice, though, was that the length of time had shortened before he was able to feel the erratic panic receding so he could breathe easier.

***

"He was telling the truth." Maya ground out the words, along with her annoyance.

"I know."

"How?"

"Intelligence training, it's pretty darn thorough."

"I bet." Maya had noticed Nik's face change just before she'd stepped in to deal with Lister. Galvanized to react, she'd motioned him to back off. But she'd been aware of the impact her brawl had made on him. Just thinking about it made her heart slip into the rhythm of a rumba, beating fast and furious.

He cared.

She'd seen it plainly. His acting all nonchalant had covered it up, but she'd sensed the toll it had taken and she wanted to wrap her arms around the man and squeeze him as hard as she had her favorite, child-sized, teddy bear that had withstood the brunt of many exuberant hugs.

It was time to relax, let go of the mad. "Wanna get something to eat and bring it to the motel? See if your buddy shows up? Maybe we'll be lucky and he'll be there."

"Maybe we'll be even luckier and he won't." Nik's steady gaze caught her eye and she didn't try to look away. Instead, heart starting to dance again, she smiled her acceptance.

Full-on seduction, the man knew how to stir it well. No playing games, he showed her clearly that he wanted her.

And she was hot, wet and ready for him too.

Taking his hand, she led him to their vehicle. "Let's hope..."

Chapter 41

Once in the room, they both breathed a sigh of relief to see that it was empty. Nik set the sushi down on the table and advanced to where Maya had kicked off her shoes and settled back, with her elbows resting on the bed.

She straightened and her hands came up. "Hold it, partner. We need to talk." Maya had this conversation with all of her lovers, not that there had been scads, but she believed it better to get the business side of the relationship over before any hanky-panky begun. That way, both parties knew what to expect from their...ah...friendship.

Nik lowered himself onto the edge of the mattress next to her and relaxed. "Okay. What did you want to discuss?"

"Do you know where Max is?" *Where did that come from?*

Shocked and defensive, Nik straightened. "Now why the hell would you ask me something like that? And at a time like this! All I want to do is get your clothes off, kiss you everywhere my lips will fit and bury myself inside that luscious body of yours and you... well, shit, I'll never understand he female mind. I thought you were with me on this."

Mad at herself for letting her tongue bypass her brain—*yet again*—she backed down from her question and apologized. "Look, for a minute there, when you were taking off your suit jacket, you looked so much like him that he popped into my mind and I didn't stop to think. I know you'd tell me if you had any information. I'm sorry." Crawling toward him, she nestled close and offered her lips in apology.

Nik pulled his head back and looked at her at the same time as he loosened his tie and undid the buttons on his shirt. "You wanted to talk. If so, you'd better say what you have to, because when I get my hands on you there'll be very little talking other than 'Oh God!', 'Now!', 'Don't stop!' and maybe 'Please!'." His smile, slow and mesmerizing, drew her into his web and she realized that there were no questions waiting, only exclamations to be uttered. Without hesitation, she started.

"Please! Now!"

Slowly he reached for her face, slid his hand under her hair and lowered his lips to hers. Teasing, he nipped at her bottom lip, then the sides of her mouth until, with a groan, he kissed her fully. Hard, then soft, and with another stifled sound, hard again, he kissed her until she felt like she was drowning in his seduction.

Her needs as strong as his, she returned his loving assault. Opening to him, she let her tongue intertwine with his in a routine as old as time. "Oh, God!" The words broke free before she could stop them and they seemed to spur him on.

Laying her backwards on the mattress, he pulled his shirt the rest of the way off then followed her down. He searched for her hands, then he lifted them above her head, holding her hostage while his lips ate at the pebbled skin of her throat, under her ears, breathing there on purpose to ramp up her excitement.

"You smell good." His voice, rough with passion, made her smile, her eyes connecting with his, loving...

"It's perfumed soap."

"I'll buy you a truckload if you use it whenever we're together."

"I wash my whole body with it."

"Oh, God!"

Undoing the buttons of her shirt seemed to take forever, but his kisses after each opening soothed her somewhat. Finally her chest was bared like his and he ground himself against her, breathing harshly, her body thrashing to bring him closer. She wanted him inside her.

His hands stroked everywhere, squeezing her breasts, fondling the nipples and caressing the skin. Parting her legs with his knee, he introduced his hard, throbbing need, his desire.

She answered by thrusting her pelvis upward, hugging him, stroking his back, his head, kissing his neck. Breathing loudly, unevenly, her whimpering sobs were probably enough evidence that she was ready for him, but just in case she added, "Yes." And then... "Please, take my pants off. Now...!" And to be absolutely sure he'd get the message, she moaned his name, "Nik! Oh God!"

That's when her cell phone rang. And two seconds later, so did Max's, which was stashed in Nik's back pocket.

He stiffened. So did she. They both groaned. *You've got to be kidding me...*

Chapter 42

Nik pulled away, put his on speaker and they both listened to the excited voice of Henry Lassiter talking fast and low. "Hey, something weird's going on at the Smith & Son office. You might want to get down here. Can you find Maya? Conley's with me and he's calling her, but she's not answering her phone."

"Sure, we're together having dinner. She's in the bathroom and her phone's here. What's up?" He reached over and rested his palm against the side of her face, then he winked.

She nodded her thanks.

"First a black SUV pulled up outside the office building and a couple of big brutes forced a young girl out of the back seat. We contemplated going in to see what the devil was going on, but before we'd made up our minds about how to handle it, we saw this smaller person in a hoodie, figured it was another girl by the build, sneaking around through the gate and into the yard. We weren't sure what we should do. The boss told us surveillance only. We didn't want to screw with someone else's ongoing investigation—you know?"

Nik watched Maya's hand signals and followed her directives. "You're doing right. Stand down and just observe. We'll be there shortly. Leave the van doors unlocked."

He pushed the off button and exhaled louder than necessary, revealing his resentment. "Oh, baby, you have no idea how much I want to say fuck it, close out the world and pull you back onto that bed. I guess it's not gonna happen, though, is it?"

Grimacing, she answered, her voice filled with disgust. "Nope!"

Shrugging, Nik stood, grabbed his shirt off the floor and stopped what he was doing to watch her putting her bra back on. Another loud sigh escaped and made her smile.

"Hold that thought, sugar. We'll get back to it later. Do you happen to have a black T-shirt I can borrow?"

"Seriously?"

"In case we have to do any snooping around. My white blouse is... " Her raised eyebrow said it all.

"Right!" He dug into his bag and pulled one out and held it up, then he changed his mind. "Julian has clothes hanging in the bathroom that will fit better. I'm sure there was a black shirt in there."

Sure enough, there was one with a big green, glow-in-the-dark, happy-faced marijuana leaf splattered over the front. Maya grinned, turned it inside out and slipped it on, sadly watching as Nik's gorgeous physique disappeared inside his own T-shirt.

Her remorseful sigh equaled his. Shaking her head in sorrow, she went to step out of the room and Nik's hands reached past her to hold the door closed.

Turning to face him, she knew her hunger for him was still obvious enough to read clearly. The rampaging desires he'd set loose couldn't be stopped by a phone call—no matter how urgent. Dammit, she wanted this man with an intensity she'd never felt before.

Gripping her head in both his hands, he kissed her hard. "Be careful tonight. My instincts are telling me something is going to happen."

"Always. You too. We still have a date for later, right?" She instigated another kiss and broke it off before it could carry them away. Then she spun around, opened the door and led the way to Max's Lexus.

"Oh, no!" Nik took two steps back, his hands up. He already had some repair work to get done on the rear bumper.

"Yes. They'll make our FBI issue, you know they will. Just get in and let's go."

"They know Max's car too."

"Not in the dark. It just looks like any car. Quit arguing and get in."

***

They arrived in record time and snuck into the reconnaissance van. Lassiter and Conley were both there, avidly watching the screen. Lassiter turned to face them with a grin. "Wow, you were right, it didn't take any time at all for you folks to get here. What kind of a diner were you at? Funny no one noticed your T-shirt was on inside out."

Conley snickered and earned a dirty look from Nik—clearly an unspoken message to wipe the grin off his face.

Maya chuckled. "Didn't think you had such good observation skills, Lassie." First she pissed off Lassiter with a nickname he hated, and then she lifted her t-shirt up to give them an eyeful of bra-clad boobs and a big green happy-face. "We stopped at a nearby place to get me a dark shirt, in case we needed to get closer. They didn't have plain ones. You satisfied?"

"Oh, yeah!" Both men laughed and nodded simultaneously.

Nik sighed. Then he spotted the video and pointed. "What have you got?"

Conley rewound the scene on the monitor, and soon Nik and Maya watched as a familiar SUV pulled up outside the entrance and two men roughly forced a struggling teen from the back seat. By her slender build, long black hair and darker skin tone, she looked to be Oriental, and the name Mai burst into Maya's conscience. Hearing Nik's exclamation, she glanced at him, and their shared look spoke what was in both their thoughts.

Soon, the tape revealed another figure breaking cover, stalking the premises, his hood pulled over his blond curls.

Juli! Maya's shock registered.

"Julian?" Nik uttered the name of the man they both recognized. "Son-of-a-bitch! What the hell is he doing here?"

"You know that person?" Conley pointed at the screen as it showed Juli disappear into the darkened yard.

"Yeah! He's my pal from out of town."

"Shit, man. I'm sorry I didn't recognize him. What the hell has he got to do with this case?"

"Beats me! He just keeps popping up at the most opportune times. Have you got anything more on video?"

"Nothing that shows what's going on down there. Hold it! Look." He pointed to the other monitor showing real time. "They're forcing those two in that truck. I think they're getting ready to leave. Maya, isn't that the same eighteen-wheeler you two have pictured on your case board? The one Al Bard got picked up in?"

"You're right! Uh-oh! The SUV is leaving too. Looks to me like they're the same two dudes who brought in the young girl. Only, they're going in the opposite direction."

Maya stopped with her hand on the latch. "You guys hang out here. Keep your eyes open, okay? We're going to tail the rig with Julian and the girl. Maybe they're going to pick up more hostages, or it could be they're shipping the ones they already have to another city. Whichever way they're headed, we'll keep you informed."

Chapter 43

Nik followed Maya to their vehicle and threw her the keys. Intuition had him heading to the passenger side. Not only did she know the district better than he did, but she also drove like a demon, there were no two ways about it. Chances were they'd need her skills. Only problem he worried about was being able to stomp down on his reactive panic if things got too crazy.

Soon as she hit the gas he knew they were in for a wild ride. Wheeling the car around, laughing with joy, she cut in and out of the traffic until they were only two cars behind the truck. "Max has never let me drive his car. No matter how much I begged."

Nik gulped and said a silent apology to his brother who, as far as he was concerned, never had to know his toy had been handled by this pro. "He was just protecting his investment."

"You mean he was a big baby. I tried every trick to get him to hand over the keys, but it didn't happen. I wish he was here now."

Nik looked out of the side windows and grinned. *Hey,*

bro, you should see her handle this ride. Ha, you'd be shitting yourself.

The squeal of the wheels caught his attention and he leaned harder on the handle near his arm. They'd followed the truck to a dark road he didn't know and there weren't any more vehicles separating them. Suddenly, out of seemingly nowhere, a black SUV crawled up beside them. Shit! He'd seen them head off in the other direction. How the hell could they turn up here?

"Looks like we have company." Maya's enjoyment sparked excitement in her cheerful voice. Their situation didn't faze her one little bit.

He watched her handling the powerful machine like she was doing what she was born to do. *Incredible! Even sexy!*

Thick red hair framed her face, revealing her profile: high cheekbones, pretty, pert nose, and lush smiling lips. Her relaxed expression made him tense more. Wasn't she taking any of this seriously? *Shit!*

Nik, on the other hand, hated not being in control and was beginning to feel the saliva building in his mouth and the bile activating in his stomach. No goddamn way would he allow this shit to catch him now. He took deep breaths and, using sheer willpower, forced back the alarm. Slipping his gun from his holster, he got ready for whatever would happen.

Meanwhile, Maya fought to keep the car on the road while the black beast seemed determined not to let that happen. Gunning the engine and having it respond with a huge burst of speed, Maya was forced to cut off the SUV and overtake the truck. The driver, not liking their shenanigans, tried accelerating also. Only the he didn't have the same skills as Maya and couldn't handle the speed. The big monster began fishtailing like crazy.

Caught beside the weaving eighteen-wheeler and the SUV forcing them there, Maya had to either speed up and take a chance on getting rammed by the swaying mass or hit the ditch. At this speed, neither was a good option.

Handling the car like a qualified NASCAR driver, she connived to keep the car under her control, using the brake, steering wheel, gas pedal, and sheer guts. Strangely, Nik began to see the game she played and enjoy watching her reactions and her sheer genius in handling the powerful vehicle.

But, unfortunately, the driver of the truck didn't have the same skills as she did. The long trailer swung out too wide cutting off the road, swerving crazily.

Forced by circumstances, Maya had no choice but to drive Max's baby over the approaching embankment.

Chapter 44

The tree that stopped their headlong descent wasn't kind to the front of the Lexus CT. However, there was no question that the quality of the manufacturing saved their lives. Surrounding airbags inflated on impact and kept them both from being killed.

Sometimes shock could hold off the pain after injuries, and Maya was sure that was what happened in her case. Calm, glad to be alive, even giddy, but nothing hurt—yet. Funny thing, the moon stung her eyes. It was bright, but also wavering and annoying.

Jerking away from the offending nuisance, she turned to Nik. "Are you okay?" She'd heard him moan and saw the terror he couldn't hide. "What's wrong?"

"Nothing. I'm fine. Just a little PTSD kicking in."

"Post-traumatic stress disorder! Holy shit. That's why you're stateside. Hold it! Do you hear what I hear? They're coming. Play dead but keep your gun handy. If they make a move to shoot, do it first."

"Shush!" This was in Nik's area of expertise. First he undid his seat belt and then hers. Slowly opening the door a crack he stopped, copied her and let his head fall forward.

Maya heard the squabbling between the men before seeing them.

"Hold that flashlight steady. Man, you got shit for brains if you think I'm crawling through that fucking swamp just to see if they're goners. You know how much bacteria lives in those infested swamps?" Whining worse than a little girl, the big dude, the same one that had lit Nik's fuse at the office, grunted his way to within ten feet of the front of the car, cussing the whole time.

"Shut up, ya big baby. You're spookin' me. Look, no-one can be alive in a smashed up wreck like that one, right? But just to be sure, I can smell the gas. You got a lighter?"

"Yeah. Here."

"Cool! I'll just light this little ol' branch, throw it on the heap and we'll be on our way."

"Good idea, Stocker. You're smart. You know Birdy's pretty shocked and says he won't drive the big rig anymore tonight."

"You kidding me? That stupid prick! How about you, Bubba? Can you drive it?"

"Nah! I don't have a commercial driver's license and I've never driven with air brakes. I warned him the boss would be pissed."

"What'd he say?"

"Screw the boss. After the ride he just survived, there's no way in hell he'll get behind the wheel again."

"Then I guess we'll have to fetch the two passengers and take them with us. The boss'll have our asses if we don't deliver the girl. They have a special customer waiting. And that little shit who's been a thorn in our sides for so long will get his later. Guess the new shipment will have to wait till morning."

Finally, the wooden stick caught and Butterball Bubba threw it where it landed in the brush next to the mangled vehicle. Before the two men reached the road, the explosion shot into the sky similar to those seen in a high-octane action movie, all fire and sparks and heat.

Stocker didn't wait to see the outcome.

Shit-for-brains ducked for no reason, then stopped to watch. "Cool!"

Chapter 45

Maya sputtered and struggled to her feet. "How the hell can you move so fast?"

"Basic training, special ops—the will to live. Sorry I had to haul you out my side. I was terrified they'd see your door open and come back to finish us off."

"Considering we just made it to the swamp before it blew, please don't apologize. In fact, I intend to make it up to you later, sugar. But now, we have to find a way to get Juli and the girl. Come on."

Checking his phone for a signal, Nik shook it with disgust and replaced it back in his pocket. "Where're we going?"

"They said Bard wouldn't drive the truck. I want to see if he really left it behind."

Apprehension lit Nik's features. Although the moon wasn't full, there was enough light for them to see their way going back up the same path their vehicle had formed on its descent. There was also enough moonshine for her to see him backing away. "Don't be a girl. I just wanted to see if there's a CB in the semi."

Relief flooded over his face and he helped her up the hill. "Good. For a minute there, I though you intended to drive it."

Maya didn't answer him. That way she wouldn't have to lie. Nor did she admit that most drivers today didn't even have CBs anymore. But some of the older models such as this ancient piece of shit did.

The same step-daddy who'd taught her how to drive, take an engine apart and hot-wire anything with wheels, had always said she handled an eighteen-wheeler better than most of the idiots on his route.

Though she'd missed the hell out of Charlie, the long-haul trucker who'd been his successor had been surprisingly kind. A braggart of a guy, Mike had liked teaching her what he knew about mechanics and there wasn't much he didn't know. Enjoying company on some of his overnight trips, if her mom hadn't wanted to travel along, Maya'd always been up for it. Her depression over losing Charlie had lifted under Mike's tutelage. He'd trusted her and she'd never let him down. Instead, her mother had taken care of that by getting caught in the sack with her next step-daddy, the Kung-Fu expert.

Nik hauled himself up the step to look inside the cab, then tried the handle. "Sorry, this baby's locked tight."

The rock she used to break the passenger window did a good job. In no time at all, she was inside the cab and checking for the phone. It was there but dead. The pigsty of a truck hadn't been looked after at all. Compared to the spotless interior of Mike's cab, this stinking, garbage heap made Maya's skin crawl. How could any driver have so little respect for such a marvelous machine?

Nik followed her to the passenger side and stood on the running board so he could see what she was doing.

Finding the right wires under the dash, in no time she'd started the engine and the roar of the motor made talking difficult. Yelling, she ordered, "Get in." Her voice brooked no refusal.

Get in? "What the hell are you talking about? You think I'm crazy—getting into an eighteen-wheeler with you behind the wheel? I'd rather jump from a helicopter with no parachute."

"Funny guy! I can drive. Get in. We need to follow that SUV. We both know the cargo is too damn precious to lose. Now get the fuck in the truck!"

"You *are* nuts. No way in hell am I getting in there with you behind the wheel."

"Fine. Then you drive."

"I can't drive one of these long-hauls."

"I can. Get in."

He stuck his hand out toward her perched behind the wheel, looking even smaller than normal—his index finger pointing at her face. It was trembling. He was shaking. Foreboding carpeted him instantly. "No Goddamned way. And nothing you say is going to convince me to get into this pigpen with you behind that fucking wheel."

Chapter 46

Slouched in the front seat of the massive, noisy semi, staring at all the various levers, lit dials, and switches, and then glaring at the busy woman driving next to him, Nik was pissed. "Threatening to withhold sex is low and just downright... mean."

"You're right. I'm *so* ashamed."

"You're *so* not funny."

"Look, I had to persuade you to give me a chance, didn't I? You want to save Juli, don't you?"

"Is that a trick question?"

"What about that young girl? Man, anything could be planned for her tonight. I've heard they hold special initiations, betting on virgins and who gets to break them in. Disgusting old men who have lots of money and no morals. If there's any way we can stop that from happening, we have to try, right?" Convincingly, she smiled his way.

"Watch the road, Maya! Jesus save me from hard-headed women." Nik lowered his arm and curled his hand into a fist. He wanted to grab at his stomach but wouldn't

give her the satisfaction of seeing his reaction to her handling of the monster she seemed able to control so easily.

"Nik, I really do know how to drive these rigs. One
of my step-daddies taught me everything he knew about
trucks, motors, and driving. You'll have to come with me
some weekend to the racetrack. It's a hoot."

God give me strength! "You race? Shit, woman, don't you
have any hobbies that aren't dangerous?"

"You mean like knitting?" The sneer was evident.

Nik had to laugh. The little minx had gotten to him
again. "No! I meant like reading and hiking, things that
aren't likely to put you in the hospital."

"Sure, I like doing both those things. I'm not the dare-
devil you seem to believe." Just then she spotted headlights
ahead and, shifting gears, the air brakes huffing, she revved
up the engine and they took off.

Nik's eyes were glued to the faded white line in the
middle of the road. *Oh, Lordie! This is not good.* Sweat broke
out, only short breaths were possible and his pounding
heart made him feel like he could pass out. *No way! That
can't happen. Maya needs me for backup. This shit's not gonna
win.* He just wished he didn't feel so weak.

Nik knew when the SUV spotted them approaching.
Of course, it *would* be just before they sped up.

"Try your cell. See if you can call for backup now.
Maybe we can get a roadblock set up further along this
stretch."

Following her directions, Nik made the call and in a
surprisingly short time, it was done. "They're heading for
the first intersection and will set up their squad cars. Five
minutes max."

"Good. They should make it. We're still ten or twelve
miles from that location. I don't want to force them to

drive too dangerously so I'm hanging back. Do you think they made us?"

"Oh, yeah! They sped up."

"There's a lot of trucks that travel this road. Look, they're slowing down again. I'll back off too. Be ready for me to pull a stunt when we have them penned in. Don't panic. I know what I'm doing." She reached her hand out to cover his. He patted hers and quickly replaced it on the wheel.

Laughing, she winked at him. "Just so you know, I can't wait to be alone with you after this is over."

"Just so *you* know, I intend to extract full compensation for the added stress you've inflicted."

"Oooh! Now I'm really excited."

"Just don't get ahead of yourself. We still have to survive the next little while in one piece."

"Hell, with that to look forward to, I'll be extra careful."

Laughing, unable to help himself, Nik felt the tenseness in his muscles ease. Then she pulled the stunt he'd been warned to watch for.

"Sh-itt!"

Chapter 47

Jackknifing a truck took skill and muscles and a whole lot of a macho. After they'd seen a similar incident, Mike had explained to her how it could be done successfully.

Sadly, the driver hadn't been able to control the skid and the truck had flipped. Since she'd never had the guts or a reason to try it before, only luck would determine if her skills were good enough.

Fighting the wheel with all the strength she could muster, Maya swung that big baby around so the semi now blocked any access to the road they'd just traveled.

It skidded and shuddered, almost flipping, but, somehow, using various levers and working the brakes, praying the tandems were set back far enough to help control the beast, she pulled off the wheelie and they skidded to a jerking stop. Dust, flying everywhere, adding a dimension of unreality to the moment.

Seconds passed before either of them moved or spoke. Nik broke the silence first. "Dammit, lady, you are amazing." In a voice a few notes higher than normal, those were the only words he uttered before they heard gunfire.

Maya saw him stiffen. Still dazed by her struggles with the eighteen-wheeler, she didn't react. But he did.

"We're sitting ducks up here." His words never registered and she didn't move.

He pulled her down in the seat and before she knew it, he'd maneuvered them out of the passenger door on his side and onto the ground. Now, weak as a kitten, having used up all her grit fighting to control the truck, she let him take over.

Carrying most of her weight, he shuffled them to a safe vantage point. Then he left her for a few seconds to do reconnaissance.

Less than a minute later, he returned, appearing out of the dark like a gliding shadow with no forewarning. "They set up two cop cars with only four officers. From what I could make out, a couple are down. Those two SUV assholes have assault weapons. Wait here. I'm going to get closer and see if I can help."

Maya nodded and slumped against the tree. Her brain felt like putty and there was very little energy left in her overtaxed body. "Okay. Give me a minute. I'll be there soon."

"No, baby. You're spent." Nik caressed her cheek to get her attention. When she focused on him, he added, "I'll take care of things. Just stay here."

In seconds, Nik disappeared. Not even the surrounding brush stirred as he slipped away. Hearing the rattling of the firing arms in the distance, Maya knew she should investigate, but the slight incline to reach the road looked like Monkey Hill. It would take more energy than she could muster.

The gunfire stopped. She sagged. Then it started up again.

She moved...

Chapter 48

Nik, aware and gratified that his training had kicked in, shifted closer to the action. Flattened on the ridge of the bank, he saw yet another cop grab his chest and drop.

With nothing left to lose the killers were obviously willing to take as many lives as necessary to get away.

Palming his gun, Nik decided his best chance was to go around through the brush and trees to get closer to the SUV from the right. He'd get a clear shot at Butterball and the other turkey. That would leave just Bard, the same idiot hiding behind the open door of their vehicle, screeching, being bloody annoying. Just then, Nik saw a man's bound hands reaching from the open window, wrap around the loser's neck and hold on. Bard struggled but couldn't break loose. Eventually, he slumped over.

Julian! Good man.

Swiftly moving into place, Nik made his way to where he'd get the best advantage for a clear shot and took it. Clutching at his stomach, Bubba hit the ground. The other gunman swung Nik's way and a round of bullets decimated much of his camouflage.

Crab-crawling, Nik worked around to the next clump of trees. From there, he could see the gunman disappearing to the other side of the vehicle.

Assessing the situation came naturally to him. Distancing himself from his rioting emotions took more effort but it paid off. He was in complete control. It felt good. Taking a few seconds, he scanned the area. Near to where he'd left Maya, he saw a dark shadow moving toward the action.

Shit! Why didn't that woman ever do as she was told? Immediately, his body's responses invaded his composure. Sweat pooled all over his body and spurts of rampant adrenaline were spiking, leaving his breathing choppy and his head reeling.

Tires screeching caught his attention. When the gunman had been focused on Nik, the last cop had made it safely into a squad car and was backing it up, trying to get away. Except, then, the road would be open for the SUV to disappear.

No fucking way he'd get back in the big rig with Maya driving. And since the other cruiser had been shot up pretty badly, if they had to follow, it would be their only choice.

Uh-uh! This had to stop now. Thinking to keep the gunman's attention on him and away from Maya, noisy on purpose, he kept zigzagging until he had the demolished cruiser for protection. Shots followed him all the way, ravaging the foliage in his wake; the panicky fool with the gun fired at anything that moved.

From the glow of the receding headlights, Nik knew exactly when the shooter realized there was someone sneaking around behind him. Breaking cover, Nik tried to draw the prick's attention away from Maya.

He knew he was visible and stayed that way just as long as it took for the douchebag to turn on him. Then he rolled to the right and fired a couple of times, but not before the gunner got off another barrage of bullets... this time toward Maya.

Suddenly, the headlights from the retreating car advanced. Seemed like the cop wasn't running away, just swinging the vehicle around to line it up and put the sniper on stage.

It worked like a hot damn. Seeing the approaching headlights baffled the prick. He ran toward the bush, trying to lose himself in the dark. Nik's bullet in the thigh brought him to the ground. And Maya arrived just in time to kick the gun away, straddle and hold the sucker until the furious officer left his vehicle and came running, handcuffs swinging.

"I'll take the bastard now, ma'am. Damn glad to see you two." He smiled up at Nik as he approached and then punched the whiner, wiggling on the ground under him. "Shut up, asshole." Another whack and the prisoner got the message and lay quiet. "I called for backup. They're coming, I can hear the sirens. There're three officers down back there who need medical attention."

Chapter 49

Taking the hint, Maya ran to the closest cop and saw that he held his shoulder and was conscious. "You okay, man?"

"I'm fine, Agent. You might want to check on Doug over there. He took one in the belly."

"Will do. Hang on. There's help coming." Maya ran in the direction he'd indicated and found a young patrolman unconscious with a gaping, bloody hole in his stomach. Quickly, she pulled off her T-shirt and rolled it up so she could put pressure on the wound to try and slow down the bleeding.

Nik soon joined her. He pointed at the other fallen officer and shook his head, sadness obvious in his expression.

Fury overrode her hope. "Dammit!"

"Bastards were determined to get away, no matter what."

"Yeah! I'm really sorry. But now the charge will be murder one. Hopefully, that'll make them talk. Maybe they'll tell us where the container is." Maya couldn't wait to drill the losers when they got them in the interview room.

"That depends on what scares them the most. And,

somehow, from what we heard earlier, I don't think they're as afraid of prison as they are of their boss."

"I can take it from here, Agent Barnes." The approaching medical team were all eyeballs and grins when they saw Maya's lacy white bra. In the dim light, the pale mounds of her breasts were obvious attractions too.

Growling, Nik quickly removed his own shirt and threw it at the unselfconscious woman. "You want those men to get anything done tonight; you might want to cover up those gorgeous tits."

Maya stood, smiled and pulled on the cover. "Thanks, partner." She chuckled when one of the EMRs whispered, "Aw!" Nik smacked the younger man on the back of the head lightly in a chummy manner, and this time she laughed. His possessiveness kind of made her feel good. Heading over to the SUV, she was glad that Nik followed.

"Is Juli okay?"

"I don't know. There hasn't been time to see. Let's go find out."

They approached the other side of the vehicle only to find a young girl with a blanket wrapped around her shoulders and her face drenched in tears.

Maya went up to her and quickly hugged the teenager, who literally collapsed in her arms. Stroking her back, rocking her, Maya whispered sweet nothings with words that sufficed in any language.

Nik caught one of the officer's attention. "Where's Julian?"

"Who?"

"Julian Freed. He was one of the hostages they'd kidnapped."

"Sorry, sir, I have no idea. We only found the girl in the car."

Son-of-a-bitch!

Chapter 50

Pulling up to Maya's house some time later, Nik hesitated to accept her invitation for coffee. He knew what would happen the minute they were alone, and he wasn't sure he should be taking advantage of her after what she'd been through earlier.

"Really? You're going to pull that shit again?"

"What shit?"

"Being all moody and rejecting my come-on." She did look a little miffed at the thought that he was seriously contemplating not taking her up on her offer.

"Look, sweetheart. There's nothing I want more than to wrap myself around... and inside that sweet body of yours. But you've been through a hell of a night. First, you were in a car accident."

"The safety bags protected us."

"Then you had to handle that damn monster truck."

"And listen to your whimpering." A soft giggle followed that fact.

"And then... you were in a shoot-out. Baby, I just don't want to act the mindless brute thinking only of myself."

Leaning into him, she let him see her globby eyes suddenly full of tears. "You know what? No one's ever been so nice to me before. I can't tell you how much it means to me."

Baffled, Nik stroked her cheek then kissed it. "What?"

"What you just said. You putting me first before your own needs." Gently, she reached for the hard protrusion between his legs to show him how aware she was of his predicament. "No one's ever done that before."

"What?" His voice lowered, a husky note creeping in.

"Cared enough to put me first. Don't you know any other word?"

"Wha—" This time she wiped his grin off with her lips.

"I want you inside. The house... and me."

Moving as only he could, Nik swung open the door of their black issue and had her in his arms, carrying her up the steps. She found the key and they entered, lips already glued to each other's.

"God, Nik. Were you really going to leave me tonight when I needed you so badly?"

"Believe me. Not because I wanted to. But you looked... I don't know... wasted." Her stiffening made him add. "I meant that in the nicest possible way. Baby, you're really drained. I saw it on the way home when you kept rubbing your hands together and then the back of your neck."

"Never too tired for you, for this..."

He kissed her hard and loved when her arms wrapped around him, pulling him closer. She was all but glued to his body, her leg encircled his hip. He adored her flexibility.

Letting her head fall back, she stared at him. He paused and looked at her. The world stopped.

They delved deep into each other's eyes, searching,

sharing—opening themselves. Their bodies melding, entwined, heart thundering against heart. It was a moment he knew was imprinted in his memory for all time, one he'd never forget. Because this was when he fell for her completely. In love, in lust—infatuated. This beautiful woman had usurped the only important thing so far in his life that he cared about—his army brothers and his career.

Nik's heart flipped open, totally vulnerable. Fear hovered waiting to take over but he wouldn't allow it access. He'd trust her.

Dear Lord, for the first time in his life, he'd believe.

His eyes filled.

Chapter 51

Maya sensed his vulnerability before she saw it. Being wrapped in his arms made her feel safe, protected... secure. Like he'd never hurt her or let anyone else do so either. The last time she'd known this feeling was when Charlie was still alive. After he'd left her alone to deal with her crazy family, she'd vowed no one would be able to get that close again. Little did she know, her heart had a will of its own.

Trust flared.

A sob broke loose.

Resisting walls, those she'd hidden behind for years, started crumbling, freeing her so she felt defenseless yet lighter, happier... in love.

He seemed to know when she'd answered his unspoken plea. Given him what he wanted from her, a promise, silent yet nevertheless binding. He groaned. It sounded like a cry of pain, yet joy gave it the lift so it made her weak with happiness.

She answered with her own weepy sigh of acceptance. Then she closed her eyes and got caught up in the sweet kiss that sealed their promise. It went on forever and drained all the negative emotions from inside, leaving only hunger for his body, passion and desire.

Her hands reached for his head, fingers skimming his face, hair, caressing his neck and keeping him in place. She never wanted this kiss to end.

Finally, breathless, their mouths slowly separated. His lips travelled to her neck and left a flurry of kisses from her hairline to her shoulders. His nuzzling aroused her to the point that her knees threatened to buckle. As if he sensed her difficulties, he swung her up into his arms and headed for the bedroom.

Once there, he laid her on the white comforter and reached over to turn on the floor lamp. While he removed his weapon and unselfconsciously stripped off his clothes, she enjoyed his performance. The man was all male, from the powerful muscles in his chest that worked their way right down his body, to the flaring hips and hard protrusion he seemed to be unaware of.

But she was. His extensive ah...asset would be the ultimate instrument to bring her great pleasure, again and again.

Leaning forward, affection overwhelming, she kissed it and he froze. Running her fingers along the length, she sucked on the tip just to let him know she liked him.

His hands in her hair, clutching then rubbing, allowed her this pleasure until he seemed overcome and gently drew her away.

"Not like this, little darlin'. My control is non-existent when it comes to you anyway, and what your lips were doing to me was pure criminal. I promise you can go back there all you want. But our first time, I'd like us both to be satisfied."

She hugged his hips, leaving one last kiss of promise, and sagged back on the bed, an arm on either side of her head. "You sure know how to break a girl's heart." Joking, she pouted and then grinned. "I'll take you up on that promise for later. But now, I feel like I need help to get undressed. You want to play lady's maid?"

Nik grinned. "Nothing I'd like better. Come 'ere, you." He hauled her tenderly to her feet and slowly worked his way through each piece of clothing, leaving kisses on every bit of skin he could reach. His day-old beard scratched in places and she never said a word, just enjoyed the sensation until he reached her tender breasts.

"I'm hurting you." Regret filled his rough voice.

"No. A little. I don't care." She angled her chest closer to his face. "Don't stop!" He took the hint. Rather than nuzzling as he had been doing, he licked and sucked the nipple – the effect was powerful.

In the meantime, his hands caressed her naked back-side, edging her closer, nestling her between his legs so he could feel her softness blanket him. Maybe he had intended to carry her to the bed, but when he lifted, she wrapped her legs around his hips, opening herself totally.

"Oh, God!"

"Please, Nik."

And so it began.

Chapter 52

Refreshed from an early morning romp, a shared shower and yet more lovemaking, Nik stopped checking his e-mails and saw that Maya was now dressed in her usual attire. Slim-fitting black pants topped with her favored embroidered white cotton blouse, and braided sandals that were just a little girlie making her look professional yet feminine. Her shiny auburn hair, lightened with streaks by the sun, framed her face in a way that he loved. He sat fully up in the bed with the sheet slipping away from his naked hips. "Now where do you think you're going, ma'am?"

Maya's eyes lingered hungrily on his body. Then she shook herself and smiled at him. "I promise I'll wait for you to come into the interview room with me when I face the shooter, but I want to hurry to the office so I can get that search warrant activated. I know you have to go to the hotel and get changed, so let's meet back at the office."

Seeing her suggestion as a sensible solution, he nodded in agreement. Accompanying her to the door, he took his time kissing her goodbye and chuckled when she started to back into the room, undoing the buttons on her blouse.

"None of that, sexy lady. There's a lot of work to get through today. Those kidnapped girls are haunting me."

She lowered her head, forehead against his chest. Leaving a soft kiss in farewell, she murmured, "I know what you mean. Okay. I'm off. Later, lover." A cheeky grin and a kiss on his nose left him reeling with affection. Not wanting to delve into the fear those sentiments generated, he grabbed for his pants.

Being alone, he took a few minutes to call Max and fill him in on what had gone down the night before.

"Bro, things are really heating up. I think it's time I returned and took up my place." Max sounded resigned.

"Can you walk very far on that leg yet?"

"It's better, man."

"Which means you can't, and I'm pretty sure running is completely out of the question."

"No matter. You're in danger. If anything happens to your ass now that Nellie's found you, I might as well shoot myself before she does it for me. You don't know our mother, Nik, or what she's capable of."

Nik laughed at the image Max set into his head. "We won't tell her."

"Nik, you won't have to. She'll know. Look, I'm on some new painkillers and they're working great. Come over later and fill me in. I'll switch back with you in the next day or so."

Nik knew bloody well that wouldn't happen. First of all, he'd never leave Maya to deal with Smith & Sons without him. And second, somewhere along the way he'd discovered feelings for his brother that wouldn't allow him to put Max in danger.

"Yeah! Fine. Gotta go. We're going to question the pricks today, and Maya is working on a warrant to search Smith's office building. We need to find their latest shipment. The semi was empty last night except for Julian and Mai, one of the teens who escaped the basement a while back with Julian's help. But we know they're out there."

"What makes you so sure there are more hostages?"

"Why would they use a semi to transport two people? Plus we overheard them talking about a shipment they were sent to pick up. Said it would have to wait until today. We need to find out what they meant. We know they do most of their monkey business at night, so if more girls were arriving to be picked up at the terminal yesterday, we better find out. It's fucking hot today and they won't last long. Look, Maya's waiting for me. I'll call later." Nik hung up and gathered the rest of his stuff.

You never told Max about his car. He should know his baby is dead. Yeah, well, sometime today, I'll call the dealer and order him a new one. Least I can do... keep peace in the family.

Grabbing a cab, Nik made it to the motel in no time at all. Thankfully, he'd moved some of Max's fancy clothes there, bought more and had what he needed to present himself at the office as his twin.

Changing quickly, he wrote another note to Julian. The last had been read and now lay crumpled on the desk. *Call me, Julian. I mean it!*

He left the number to the burner phone he and Max had set up, then started for the door. That's when he heard the key in the lock.

Julian looking beaten and exhausted entered, moving slowly. His blond curls were sweat-mangled and his face bruised and puffy. Dried blood from various cuts gave him the look of a man put through the ringer.

As soon as he saw Nik, his demeanor changed but he showed no surprise at seeing him. His impertinent manner reappeared. "Hey, sugar. You finally came home."

"Look who's talking. Where did you disappear to last night?" Nik didn't take his eyes off the man for one second. He'd known the dude wasn't who he portrayed, but dammit, he hated being played. And this sucker had played him from the first moment they met.

Nik watched Julian's expression change from his usual brazen impudence to somber. "You know I couldn't stick around, man. I told you the police were after me."

"Yeah! They wanted to talk to you, ask you some questions, is what you told us before. So rather than answer a few questions, you'd prefer to walk twenty miles back to town? Makes no sense, Julian. And you know it."

"Who said I walked? I called a friend to pick me up."

"There was no signal where we were."

"There was about a mile up the way."

Sighing, Nik changed tack. "Tell me why you followed Mai to the Smith & Sons office."

"You know about that? Okay, she's a friend of mine. Remember I told you about letting the girls free? Well, Mai stayed with me instead of running. She had no one to go back home to and didn't want to leave the States. I was trying to get some help for her from a friend."

"You mean the friend who came to pick you up?"

"No. From my boss who cares about these girls and organizes their passages home."

"Okay, so how did Mai get snatched again?" Nik wished he knew the exact questions to ask. Maya would have.

"They were trailing *me*, wanting payback for the trick I pulled at the Pink Pussycat. Mai didn't know. She came to find me because she'd heard that another girl from her village had disappeared and wanted me to help her. It was pure bad luck them seeing her on the street. They captured her just as I came around the corner and saw it happen. I was only trying to get her free."

Nik had to know. "What will happen to her now that they have her in custody?"

"I think she can apply for a domestic working visa. And since she was brought here against her will, we were hoping they would grant it to her without too much trouble."

"Okay, that makes sense. I have one more question. How the hell do you always know where I am?"

Julian began to laugh. "For a guy who prides himself on being observant, sometimes you miss what's going on right under your nose."

"What the fuck are you talking about?"

"You know Bob, the homeless man who parks himself outside the hotel? He thanks you for always dropping a few bucks in his can. Says you're one swell pecker. His words not mine."

"Bob? The creepy dude with black teeth wearing grubby army camouflage rejects? The one who talks about how stinkin' hot it always is? Makes a guy feel sorry for him?"

"That's him. Trust me. There aren't many who give a shit. You, on the other hand, always leave him a few bucks and, because of that, he'd walk through shit for you."

Understanding dawned. "So he's an informant and tells you when I'm here."

Julian started laughing. "Sugar, the man works for me. He's out there as a guard. Look closer next time you see him. Things aren't always what you expect. Max would have made him in a minute."

"Shit! This jungle just isn't my playground. Guess I have a lot to learn."

"Hey, you've done an incredible job so far. Riding to the rescue last night was spectacular; put hearts in my eyes when I saw you in your element."

"Yeah, yeah! No stroking! I want to meet your boss."

"So you've said."

"When?"

"I'll let you know."

"I can trust you?"

"Haven't I showed you that already? In the meantime, I've got to hit the shower and catch a few hours. "

"And I've got to go and catch a killer."

Chapter 53

Maya paced the office, wondering what had happened to Nik. The warrant proceedings were now set in motion and who knew how long the desk-jockeys at the courthouse would require before they'd be ready to be picked up. Hoping to speed things along, she'd gone to the boss for help in pushing it.

"I'll get them moving on the warrant," Ron had said, "but I gotta ask...You know what you're doing with this one, Agent?"

"Yes, sir. Everything we can. I appreciate you giving the go-ahead to Lassiter. It's good to have eyes on the place."

"I agree. It's why you got it. Just so you know, the brass is riding me hard me on this case. It's an international embarrassment. Since you're the one in the field, I'm passing the pressure on to you and Max. Don't let me down."

"No, sir. We're on it."

"You'd better be. Go do your job."

Leaving his office still in one piece, she accepted that she'd done everything she could to get authorization to snoop through Smith's files. Policy procedures took their own sweet time.

Waiting for Nik, she'd decided to take another run at Birdy Bard and was met with a nervous, frightened criminal and the same crafty lawyer who had rescued Smith Senior's ass the day before. "If you promise us a deal, we might be willing to share."

Not intending to play their silly games this time, Maya started, "I need you to know one important factor that might cut your client some slack. We realize he didn't have a gun and he never shot anyone. If I remember correctly, he spent most of the time unconscious. And that could play in his favor. But don't kid yourself, he will do time... Unless he can tell me about the container he was to pick up last night. The number and which ship delivered it? If he was willing to share that information, I, personally, will see to it that his assistance is taken into consideration when it comes time to plea-bargaining. "

Whispering—along with muttered arguments and hand gesturing followed. Maya watched closely and knew there would be no help here. Birdy didn't know the answers.

Meanwhile, they had one of the killers, John Stocker, from the night before, in the interview room, sitting, sweating—waiting to be questioned. She itched to get in there, but she'd made a promise to Nik.

Finally, to pass the time, she picked up the phone and called the hospital. Butterball, as he'd been affectionately dubbed by Nik the night before, but whose real name was Bubba Jones, was still there under guard and she checked to see when they figured he'd be ready to answer some questions. The nurse was almost positive the doctor would give her clearance, but he wouldn't be available to sign off on it until after lunch. Since Maya intended to be busy the rest of the morning, it worked for her.

As she lowered the phone, a coughing noise caught her attention. Becky trounced in, frustration apparent by her attitude and in her expression. Slumping in the only chair not covered with files, she pouted and then griped.

"I've been going through every avenue I can think of to come up with a manifest from Maurice's brother, Lee Smith's company, Lee Electrical, out of Singapore. I've pursued every container he's shipped for the last week and I've come up with zilch. Then I ran a search for any of the businesses listed in the holding company that Smith & Sons are connected with and that was a bust also."

"Sweet Jesus, Becky. If those girls arrived yesterday, they're running out of time."

"I know. It's why everyone is working so freakin' hard to try and find a lead. Do you have any idea how many containers enter that terminal every day from all over the world? It's like looking for one specific diamond in a trunkful."

"Shit!"

"You can say that again. It's been a real slog. I've even gotten help from a few of the others who are better at the computer than me, and still nothing."

"Becky, get real. There's no one better than you. If you say there aren't any containers arriving in New Orleans from Lee Electric then... hold it!"

"Hold what?"

"They aren't arriving in New Orleans. That's why they were taking the truck. They were going to make the pickup at another terminal. What's the closest one from here?"

"Port of South Louisiana is a huge terminal. It's one of the biggest in the western hemisphere. I'd say we're about an hour's drive."

"The sneaky bastards. Could it be possible?"

"I'm on it!" Energy renewed, Becky flew to her feet and headed for the door in time to meet up with Nik.

"Hey, ladybug." Nik greeted the girl and looked shocked when she placed a big smooch on his cheek before commenting. "You can charge me with sexual harassment, or just accept that I'm nuts about your partner and don't like kissing women. In case she isn't listening, tell her for me, she's one super-good detective."

Nik's comical expression made Maya laugh. Or was it the humming in her brain that spoke volumes. They were onto something. She just knew it.

"Should I even ask?" Nik pointed at the departing computer whiz.

Taking her time, Maya told Nik what they'd stumbled onto. Hearing him add his admiration for her quick thinking made her stammer and find her cheeks warming.

"It was a... a reasonable conclusion, not rocket science."

"True. But you thought of it and others didn't. That makes you one of the FBI's brainiest, and I might add—hottest, commodities."

"Sugar, you can quit your sweet-talking. You're already booked in for special treatment tonight. By the way, what took you so long getting here?"

Nik brought her up to date on his discussion with Julian, leaving out the parts that made him uncomfortable. Especially about destitute old Bob, the snoop he'd never even noticed.

"So now you realize that Juli *isn't* a gay dancer who helped some girls one night. Could have told you that a long time ago."

Nik crossed his arms, the jacket of his light gray suit

stressed from his bulging muscles. "Then why didn't you?"

"Cause when I ran a search on him, Julian Freed didn't exist."

Chapter 54

"Melee, will you let us have some water now? It's been hours and it's so hot, I'm having difficulty breathing." Kanya had finally stopped crying hours ago and now lay in abject misery in a fetal position on her mattress.

"She wants to keep it all for her and her little friend." Sneering, Vanida, a tall girl whose mouth had already begun to show lines from always wearing a frown, tormented Melee like she'd done from day one.

Because Melee had taken over leadership, the malcontent had argued, belittled, stirring the pot and getting the others riled. She started another harangue once again. "You are fooling the others with your loving attention, bitch, but you don't fool me. All you care about is yourself."

"That's not true. If I hadn't stopped everyone, the food would have been gone the first day and so would've the water." Melee tried to make them all see the truth. Earnestly, she stared from one to the other. "I've done it f-for you, to keep you well. Other than Solada, not one of you has tried to help."

"What is there to do? Pass out the food, of which I'm sure you keep more for *yourself* than you share amongst the rest of us." Malicious and vindictive, Vanida stressed the word to get her meaning across.

"You know that isn't true, Vanida." Calmly, Melee turned and surveyed the faces of the other girls all showing interest in the outcome of the newest battle. "I've kept the food beside me to protect everyone's portions and you've all watched whenever I've gone into the supply. The only other reason I touch the boxes is to get the mulch to add to the toilets, and as bad as the stench is, without me adding that, we would all have been poisoned by now."

"Oh, you're just *so* perfect, aren't you?" Screaming now, Vanida's hand struck Melee, sending her head reeling to the side.

With a cry of alarm, Solada, the youngest, stood to protect her friend, only to fall to the floor.

Melee pushed Vanida backward so she could bend over the child. She cradled her and stroked her head. "She's burning up." Swinging around, Melee searched for the last bottle. "We must give her the water."

Kanya spoke up. "She can have my share."

"Mine too." The others piped up and added their agreement. Worried about the youngest, they circled around the girl who'd won everyone's heart with her kindness and pretty songs that had kept them all amused during the long, dark hours.

With Kanya's help, Melee gently carried Solada to her own clean mattress and laid her down. She poured a small amount of the water into a cup and held it to the girl's lips, forcing much of it into her mouth. Then she undid the girl's blouse and wet a cloth to hold against her overheated skin.

Melee had no real nursing experience, but she sensed that Solada was in real trouble. She wasn't just dehydrated, there was something else affecting her.

Murmurs of affection and worry circulated the group and caught her attention. "Someone will come soon. You know we have landed. The small windows at the top of the container now show the blue sky, rather than the darkness from being inside the ship."

Kanya added. "Yes, and since the last few hours, there's slightly more fresh air. Has anyone else noticed it? Maybe we should try yelling again for help?"

Vanida piped up from the corner where she'd retreated. "Who has any voice left? None of us can speak above a whisper anymore, we're so dry. And you're giving all of our water to that brat."

Before Melee could respond, four others turned on the complainer. "Shut up, Vanida. You haven't stopped whining since we woke up in this hellhole."

"We don't want to hear it anymore."

"We must all stick together."

Vanida, pushed to her limits, broke down and howled. "Do you know what they plan on doing to us? We'll be forced to be prostitutes, letting any disgusting man do what he wants. And there'll be nothing we can do about it. I hate men. I'd rather be dead."

Melee's soft voice answered with a phrase that everyone had heard all their lives. "What will be, will be."

Chapter 55

John Stocker was a true psychopath, high-functioning and clever.

Maya had only met one before, but she knew it immediately after they entered the interview room. His aura was a thick gray veering on black, and his reptilian eyes were windows into a heartless soul.

Shivers of apprehension raced over her body, and she looked to see if the surrounding negative energy was affecting Nik and saw that it was. Rather than his customary lounging, her partner's arms were crossed and he stood close, ready.

Ignoring the voice in her head that told her to get the hell out of there, she pulled out the chair across from the smiling man, placed her files on the table between them and closed the buttons on her light jacket.

"Hello, Agent Barnes. How nice of you to come and speak to me personally."

"This is no friendly visit, Mr. Stocker. I have a few questions I'd like you to answer."

"Ask them. If I can help you, sweetheart, it'll be my

pleasure."

Maya glanced at Nik with a distinct warning in her stare. *Don't let him play you.*

"Oh, you can answer them all right. But will you? For instance, who is your boss?"

"Next question."

"Where were you going last night?"

"Pass."

"Why did you shoot those officers?"

"Because they were there. Next."

"You're having fun, aren't you?"

"Yes. I am. I don't get to visit with a sexy woman like you very often. And when I do, they certainly aren't wasting time asking me stupid questions."

"Agent Foster!" Maya held her hand out toward Nik to stop his obvious intention of defending her. The ice in his pale blue eyes reminded her of a picture she'd once seen of an Alaskan glacier: cold, bitterly cold.

Feeling as if filth had seeped into her pores and only a long, hot shower with disinfectant soap would ever make her feel clean again, but remembering the hostages, Maya persevered. "Mr. Stocker, this may be a joke to you, but it's very important to us that we find a container Mr. Bard was sent to collect last night. If you could please tell us about it, we'd look kindly on that help as a reason to—shall we say—make special arrangements with the prosecuting attorney."

"If those special arrangements would include a night alone with your luscious body, I'd be sorely tempted to answer. As it is, I don't believe that will ever happen. Therefore, Agent Bitch, I regretfully decline your generosity."

Incensed eyes filled with disgust, Maya stepped in

front of Nik before he could touch Stocker. Leaning closer to the sicko, she spoke softly. "Your poor mother must have hated you."

When the animal lunged, Nik moved. The old saying about greased lightning came to Maya's mind when he dove between her and the hands reaching for her throat. One backhand with the power of his arm behind it had Stocker, who was much smaller, flying against the wall.

Just then the door flung open and two burly officers rushed in to control the raging beast. Subdued and hand-cuffed, they pushed the furious fiend out of the room.

"I'd say that went well." Maya's trembling hands lifted her hair off her neck as she crossed her fingers at the back of her head.

"What did you say to him?" Nik went toward her, then hesitated. She sensed him stopping and waiting.

"Something I'm not too proud of. He pissed me off and all I could think of was those poor little girls in the hands of such an animal." Maya dithered about sharing with Nik how low she'd stooped but then thought better of it. He had to realize she had a temper. If he still wanted to be with her after he learned what she was capable of when angry, it might mean he could care for her no matter what. And maybe he'd stay the course, not leave like her step-daddies had done all her life.

Besides... if her behavior scared him off, so be it. She didn't want a weak man who couldn't take the hard in her along with the soft.

Chapter 56

By her behavior, Nik sensed they had come to some kind of a milestone. When Maya hesitated to tell him what she'd said that had set Stocker off, he didn't push—just waited. He'd seen her anger, felt the bristling energy that had lit her fuse. In her job, he knew there were many days when the fury simmered. And normally, she kept it controlled. It was what he admired about the woman—her total professionalism.

Yet there was a side of her that was all female softness and loving heart. Her hesitation made him worry. Set his heart to beating faster and the bile in his stomach to start seething.

She finally admitted, "I'm ashamed for playing his game."

When she confessed to what had inflamed Stocker, he felt nothing but pride for the fact that she'd had the balls to stand up to the creep.

What worried him the most was her choosing the one conviction that had followed him all his life. His father had hated *him*. Had he been so unlovable? Suddenly, rather than accepting the fact—he questioned the reason and came up with a truth that lightened his spirit.

It had nothing to do with him... never had.

It was his father's disability. The man had been a psychopath, the same as their prisoner. And Nik wasn't anything like him, never could be. He had a heart. He loved.

Like a caterpillar escaping the imprisonment of his self-made cocoon, Nik shed the fear that had shadowed him every day. Acceptance flooded in; he was nothing like that wicked Bastard, he was normal and could have what other men cherished—a future with a wife and babies, a home of his own.

Peace descended and made him feel lightheaded.

"Nik.... Hey, partner!"

Calling him "partner" as she'd begun to do at the office, so as not to let the cat out of the bag, Maya had to speak twice to get his attention. He read the anxiety in her eyes and knew instantly what had put it there.

"Maya, I was thinking about what you said and how it reminded me of my old man. He hated me too and being his son was a nightmare. If Stocker had a mother like him, I almost feel pity for the little boy. But no blasted way in hell do I feel sorry for a grown man who chose to be a waste of skin. So, don't be afraid that I'll look down on you for losing it. I admire that you even took him on."

"Truly? You had me worried when you didn't say anything. I'm far from perfect, sugar. But I'll never leave if you give me good reasons to stay."

Unconsciously, he reached for her and stopped when she put her hands on his chest to hold him off. "Keep that thought, Baudin. Always..."

Chapter 57

Butterball was not a good patient. The nurses's disgust at his shenanigans was obvious. As Nik and Maya entered the room and they were leaving, the smaller girl muttered, "Stay back. The brute has the brains of a flea and the manners of a horny dog. They should put handcuffs on both of his arms."

Maya approached him first and saw what they meant when his hard fingers encircled her wrist to pull her down. Wrenching away, she did a reverse move on him and in seconds had his arm twisted backwards in a painful hold.

"You want to play, asshole? Keep it up and I'll let Agent Foster at you again. I see the bruises haven't healed from your last dance with him."

"What the fuck do you two want here? I have nothing to say to either of you schmucks."

Sensing his withdrawal, Maya dropped his arm and wiped her hands on her pant legs. "You might change your mind once I tell you that Officer Fred Stoles died from a bullet shot from your gun. That means murder one, Bubba. And Louisiana still believes in capital punishment.

You know, the death penalty: uncomfortable chair with leather straps, lethal injections – the whole package. And you a cop killer." Maya grinned at Nik without a hint of real amusement. "What do you think, Agent Foster? How much mercy you figure the judge and jury are going to show Bubba here?"

"I heard Officer Stoles had two small children, and his wife is pregnant with the third. That little woman's going to get a whole lot of sympathy. Personally, I figure Bubba here is cooked meat."

"My take, also. You're going to need a miracle, Mr. Jones, and that's what I've come to offer. A miracle. You interested?"

"Hell yeah! Are you talking a reduced sentence?"

"Life, yes. But not death."

"What do you want to know?"

Realizing the weasel had no allegiance to his boss or the boys in his gang, Maya's glee fought a battle with disgust. Hadn't the man ever heard of honor amongst thieves? Before he could change his mind and lawyer up, she went straight to the point. "We need to find out which container Bard was going to pick up last night. The terminal and, if possible, the number on the box."

Bubba's expression became belligerent. "How the fuck would I know that?"

, "You were there."

"Because Birdy called us and said he was being followed. The boss warned us he needed that Oriental squeeze for some customers he'd lined up. And that other dude, trying to save his girlfriend, had a date with the swamp. As far as any containers, I got nothing."

Misery blanketing his face gave the whole story; Maya instinctively knew that he was telling the truth. If the asshole had something, *anything*, he'd spill his guts to save his hide.

"Do you happen to know if Smith ever has pick-ups at any other terminals? Like the Port of South Louisiana?"

"Sure. We get cargo from everywhere. Some comes by rail, but most of it by ship. He sends the trucks every few days to get the pick-ups."

"They must have some of the employees at the terminal on their payroll."

Bubba looked at her like she was daft. "Well, of course."

"So they make pick-ups at night?"

"Sometimes. But only for the special freight."

"By special freight, you mean the girls."

"Yeah. Except that I heard the boss on the phone with his brother. They were arguing. Moe wanted the deliveries to continue, but Lee said they weren't sending more girls until things calmed down. The boss is pissed with the amount of interference there's been lately."

"So the container coming in now was to be the last for a while?"

"I guess. But I don't know nothing about its arrival time or where it'll land."

"Then you're no help to us." Maya straightened from where she'd been leaning against the bed's railing and turned to leave.

"But I'll still get my deal, right? I've got a lot of shit to share about the Mosleys. You'll want to hear it all."

"When the time comes, let's hope it leads to a conviction. Who knows, the District Attorney may be in a good mood."

Chapter 58

"Mai? It is you, I wasn't sure. You look different with your hair pinned up." Maya, rushing from the elevator, caught up with the pretty Oriental girl who lingered by the hospital's front door.

"Hello, Agent Barnes, Agent Foster. How are you today?"

"Just peachy. And please call us by our first names. I'm Maya, and this is my partner, Max. More important, how are you?"

"Thank you, Maya. I'd be delighted. And I am better."

"Did the doctors discharge you already?"

"Yes. They have nothing to keep me here for. I just hesitate to step outside in case those creeps are watching the building. It hasn't been safe on the streets of New Orleans for me."

Nik spoke up. "I know, Julian told me about them picking you up last night. That must have been terrifying."

Mai looked at Nik, confusion covering her pretty face. "Julian? I'm afraid I don't understand. I don't know anyone called Julian."

Nik's antennae bristled and he talked slower. "Julian Freed, the blond man who was with you in the truck."

"Oh, you mean Justin. Yes, he's been wonderful. I'm going to meet him now."

Maya's intuition kicked in. She understood that Nik was onto something and wanted to help. "Sweetie, let us drive you to where you need to go. That way we'll all be happy. Nik and I will know you're safe, and you can relax and tell us all about where you're from."

"I'd be happy to accept a ride with you. Thank you." Mai's face brightened and her nervousness faded.

Maya stepped in front of the girl as a precaution before exiting the building. She'd caught Nik's beam of approval and sensed he would have spoken if she hadn't. It was nice to be so in tune with her bogus partner.

Soon, with Nik at the wheel and Maya sitting in the back with Mai, they were driving along according to her instructions. "I'm sorry I don't know the house number, just the street."

"That's fine, sweetie. We'll get you close and you can point out the house. Now tell us what happened last night."

"I was going to meet with Justin. I'd just found out from a friend in my village that another girl had been taken. Solada's very young, only thirteen. She's delicate also. I'm very worried about her. I know how difficult the journey in the container from Singapore was—the girls fighting, the lack of food and water, it was dreadful—a nightmare."

"I'm sorry you had to go through something so horrible, Mai. Since you're rather petite, I'm sure you were one of the girls who suffered more."

"No, I was lucky to have a guardian angel who protected me."

Thinking she meant the words figuratively, Maya patted her hand. "I'm glad." She smiled at the girl and saw her fingering a locket. A hunch made her hesitate. She caught Nik's glance in the mirror and knew he'd picked up on it too. "Who was your defender, Mai?"

"Her name was Tina, actually Christine. She was my savior. Never once did she let the others steal from me or hurt me. And there were many terrible battles; fear drove the others crazy. But Tina kept me safe with her and we shared our portions with each other. I loved her. When the men came to take us away, she managed to run and hide from them. She promised to get help for us. I'm so sorry she had to die the way she did." Tears filled Mai's eyes and she quickly swiped at them with her fist.

Maya spoke softly. "She was very brave and she left us a message about you. We've been searching for you because of what she wrote."

Eyes glowing, Mai nodded. "Justin told me."

"He told you she was locked inside one of the containers?"

"Yes. I wish she would have stayed with us. She'd be free now. Turn here, Nik. The house is just before next corner."

Maya glanced around her and a niggling feeling grabbed hold. The houses looked familiar and she knew the next street very well.

Nik pulled over to the curb and got out of the car. He opened the back door and helped first Maya and then Mai out before looking around. His head swiveled to Maya and his eyes questioned.

Mai noticed the tension. "Is there something wrong?"

Maya answered. "Max's mother lives near here."

Chapter 59

What the...? When Mai led them up the familiar stairs of Nellie's house, a swarm of questions rattled Nik's brain. How could his mother be involved with the kidnapped teens? He glanced along the street at the neighboring double-gallery homes, modest constructions built in the 1850s, the intricate balconies filled with greenery, vines and blooms. His mother's house had struck a chord deep within and he'd researched its history.

Mai rang the doorbell again and they waited.

Finally, Nellie appeared, smiles lighting her face until she saw Mai. Then a wary expression settled. "Nik... son, I must give you a key so you don't have to ring the doorbell. Please, come in."

Nellie's arms were open and, without knowing how it happened, he walked into them to get his hug.

Son! Somehow that small word started a glow inside that he wanted to hide and cherish, even from Maya. *Christ, you're a needy bastard.*

Once the greetings with Maya and Nik were finished, Nellie turned to Mai. "Hello child. I'm sorry I couldn't pick you up from the hospital. We have a crisis today and I couldn't leave the phones."

"Nellie, I think—"

Nellie rounded on him and slapped his arm lightly. "You will call me Mom, Maman, Mother, or—heaven forbid—even Ma, but you will not call me Nellie. Understood?"

Feeling sheepish, Nik found himself grinning like an idiot. "Okay, Mommy dearest, are you up to answering all the questions that Maya is dying to ask?"

Laughing, Nellie said. "Not until I get the coffee organized. "Justin, you might as well come out now. I believe the gig is up." Nellie turned to Nik and Maya. "You know him as Juli or Julian."

Julian! Justin? What the...? Nik couldn't seem to bring himself to even think cuss words when he was near to his mother. Somehow, it seemed wrong but he sure as f*** wanted answers.

As they followed Nellie to the cooler dining room, Maya gave Nik a secretive wink and slid her hand into his for a few seconds. She sensed his anxiety and he loved her for her perception. They took their seats around a large oval table that resembled one most often seen in a boardroom. In fact, the whole set-up seemed strangely like one might find in an elite office building.

The door to the right opened and Julian appeared, looking like a refreshed replica of the man Nik had seen that morning. This dude didn't sway his hips or wave his hands; rather he looked ordinary, wearing clothes even Nik would choose. He took a seat across from Nik and leaned back in his chair, totally relaxed. "Mina's bringing the coffee."

Nellie noticed the questioning looks and added.

"Mina's my housekeeper. I've had her since my sister, Vi, passed on. She gives me the time and freedom to do my real work as CEO of Harkins Security."

Maya recognized the name from having lived in New Orleans for so many years, but Nik was lost. "You run a company? Your own company? Max never said anything."

The smell of hot coffee and biscuits permeated the air seconds before big, beautiful, black Mina arrived with the tray. Both Nik and Justin jumped up to help and ended up with a tug of war that Nik won. Justin backed off with a chuckle. "All yours, sugar."

Nik faked a growl, placed the tray in front of his mom and resumed his seat. "About this company that *even* my brother doesn't seem to be aware of...?"

Nellie assumed a sly look and had trouble meeting his gaze. "Max never really understood how involved I had become over the last few years. Don't get that look, Nik. He was busy building his own career with the FBI. And...he had enough sense to know I didn't need to be babysat like some old bat with no brains. He respected my independence." Nellie slid the tray to Mai. "Could you pass the coffee around, Mai honey? Thanks."

"So noted." Nik smiled gently. "Sorry. Continue."

"When my brother-in-law, Ed, died, he'd left a real mess. The lazy ass didn't like working though his father had left him a well-run organization. His managers were robbing him blind and Vi couldn't have cared less. All she wanted was to lie around, watch her soap operas and eat bonbons." Nellie spat out the last words, disgust ringing clearly in the dry tone she used. "Someone had to step in. One of the younger men in the company, a smart, honest, hard-worker who knew what was going on—"

"Don't forget good-looking." Justin bowed.

"Ugly as sin smart-ass came to me and showed me proof of what was happening to the business. So I made a deal with my sister."

"Blackmailed her, you mean." Justin laughed. "Thank goodness."

Nik looked from one to the other and sensed a camaraderie he'd had with some of his own men. His respect and liking for the blond stalker grew.

Sheepishly, Nellie agreed. "She got to keep her lifestyle and I got the company. She signed it over to me lock, stock, and barrel. Her only dictate was that I had to stay home and look after her. Which, as you know, I did. Turned out she did me a great favor. Once I'd learned how to use the computers—had a private tutor for months—I set up an office here in Ed's old bedroom and ran the company with Justin's help. But it's grown so large now, I'm getting lost."

Did her voice weaken on purpose? Nik could have sworn a pathetic tone became noticeable. He glanced at Justin and saw him lower his head to hide a grin. "I need someone who I respect, a strong *man* to take over. With Max out of the picture..."

Now Nik's antennae really picked up signals. Did she know about Max? It didn't seem so important now to keep Max's secret, but Nik respected that it wasn't his to share. He kept his mouth shut.

Maya had sat quietly throughout the tale, but she now leaned forward in her chair and spoke to Nellie. "You're the person who's been helping the freed girls?"

"Yes. We've arranged passage for them, getting them back to their people."

"Juli... Justin was working for you. How did he know about the Pink Pussycat?"

"Sometimes Max and I would talk about his cases."

More 'n likely, Nellie would probe and Max would share. Nik knew it. He glanced at Justin and saw that he'd picked up on Nik's comprehension. The miniscule nod was enough for Nik to know he'd hit on something.

"Max had mentioned that he thought there was a link to Smith & Sons because their employees often hung out at the joint. Justin followed up that information by appearing there, dancing and talking to their girls. It paid off."

"But how did you know that Smith & Sons were the culprits?"

"Because Max's snitch worked for us. He did pass out the night he saw Max get beaten up. But not because he'd taken bad drugs like he told the cops. The bastards clobbered him after he tried to stop them beating up Max. Stupid idiots hadn't searched him so the files he'd had to pass on were still intact."

"*You* were passing on information to help in our case?"

"Yes. We were running a parallel investigation, hoping to stop those shipments. We had a client whose niece had been one of the girls taken hostage: Christine Ramos, the girl who died. They were willing to pay us to continue searching, which we would have done anyway. The thought of what they planned for those poor babies sickens me. I was prepared to do anything to stop it from happening."

Maya assumed a thoughtful expression that Nik noticed immediately.

"A while back, there was a club full of young, foreign prostitutes that had recently been raided, the girls were released and then disappeared..."

"The ones you believed had been taken by a rival gang?"

"Those're the ones."

"Yes, they've all been returned to their families."

"And you didn't see the need to go through legal channels like the FBI?"

"And suffer all that red tape you guys are so fond of?"

Obviously not willing to push buttons that couldn't be undone, Maya switched to another topic. "Do you know where Max is?"

Nellie's face underwent a complete transformation. "No. That's the one piece in the puzzle that has eluded me so far. With all of my resources, I haven't been able to find my own son."

Seeing his mother's pain, Nik knew she wasn't aware that Max was alive and well. She believed him missing and most likely dead.

His conscience tugged away, almost forcing him to breach Max's confidence. But at the last minute, he hung back. He'd have to get his brother's permission first.

Max had known that Nellie would be frightened and saddened, and yet he hadn't bothered to let her know he'd survived. Why that was, Nik didn't know. Could be that at the beginning, he'd been in such poor shape; he had no awareness of anything. Once so much time had passed, he might have wanted to protect Linda and thought the fewer people who knew he was alive, the less it was likely that any of Smith's people would find out.

It made a crazy kind of sense, but he'd still have a long talk with his twin next time he saw him.

Chapter 60

When both Nik and Maya's phones rang, they each excused themselves and went to the front room. Maya's grin of gladness matched the one he was sure was plastered on his face. He couldn't help himself. Leaning down, he kissed her hard. "You're beautiful."

"And you're cheesy. I love it! Let's go."

They had a green light to hit the offices of Smith & Sons. The search warrant had been issued.

They returned to the dining room to say their goodbyes. Though Nellie smiled sweetly at Maya, it was Nik who she approached. While she hugged him tightly, she whispered. "Be careful. I need you. Don't take any chances."

"Don't worry, Mom. I'll be back." He looked around to say his goodbyes to Justin and noticed the dude had pulled one of his famous disappearing acts again. *Son-of-a-b... gun!*

By the time Maya and Nik had picked up the warrant and organized the troops, it was dark. Becky's group hadn't made any leeway on finding the container and, working overtime; tempers were high in the office. Everyone knew that those girls only had so much time left before they all ended up like Tina. They needed to know which terminal held the precious cargo and the number of containers at those places was in the thousands.

Assistant to the Special Agent in Charge, Maya and Max's boss, Ron Bitters, had even sent troops to walk the yards, dogs on leashes and heat scanning sensors. But the terminals were plenty and vast. It took time.

Maya called Lister who was still on surveillance. "What's going on there, Henry?"

"It's been quiet, Maya. They're still working, lights are all on. Smith hasn't left the premises all day, or his son. Some of his men have vamoosed and come back. We had them followed by plain-clothes and nothing interesting has happened. What's going on with your end?"

"We just got the go-ahead. We'll be there soon with the paperwork. "

"Good. I'm sick of this post. Want to get back to the office and fresh coffee... Wait, something is happening! A car just pulled up and... son of a bitch! They have Max. He's struggling... shit, they clobbered him! I thought he was with you?"

"Are you positive it's Agent Foster?"

"Absolutely positive."

Chapter 61

Nik! Oh, God. Maya's heart started beating harder, faster, making breathing impossible. They'd needed vests and she'd sent him to Max's locker to get his. She thought he'd been gone a mite too long, figured he'd needed help to find the way. Occupied with so many details, the time had passed and she hadn't paid attention.

Running, not stopping to think or even blink the tears from her eyes, she yelled out orders to the others and took off.

Her car spun out of the garage, leaving black rubber and smoke, and all she could think of was to get that five-mile drive over with so she could be near him, save him. *Nik!*

The screaming of her car's siren, fool-hearted dashes across crowded intersections, shaking foot hard on the accelerator, all rivaled the surges of adrenalin that spiked her system. The minutes passed in a fog of tears and prayers. *Now that she'd found the one man who could make her life worthwhile, how the hell could she live without him? God! Please!*

The only reason she came to her senses before she'd driven right into the yard, pulled her gun and badge then forced her way in was her fear of what they would do to Nik. *No crazy stunts!* If she had any chance of saving his life, she needed to play this smart—legal paperwork, a backup team and the law on her side.

Fuck they cared about the law? The idea took hold and wouldn't shake loose. She pulled up and parked two vehicles behind the surveillance van, exited the car, and skulking, worked her way to the back door. She knocked softly, calling for Higgins to let her in. No answer prompted her to try the handle and she found it open.

In seconds, she knew why there'd been no response. Higgins, slumped over the monitor with a bullet in the back of his head, wouldn't be any help whatsoever. Until her team arrived, she had to go it alone.

Suddenly, a shot rang out from the direction of the office. It had her head swivelling and her feet moving. Screw the team. Nik needed her now!

Chapter 62

Where the hell was Maya? Nik had searched everywhere, checked the boss's office, had even gone as far as getting one of the females coming out of the bathroom to go back inside and see if she was there.

"Becky, have you seen Maya?" The approaching agent, loaded with paperwork and looking harried, nodded. "Yeah, she ran out of here a few minutes ago, crying. Never seen her look so rattled. She didn't say anything. Figured she'd gotten word on the container. I've been sick ever since."

Nik fingered his uncomfortable vest, panic flaring. *Why hadn't she waited for him?* "Doesn't make sense, she wouldn't leave without me."

"She did. Heard the squealing tires of her car all the way in here. The boss'll have her ass for that. He's chewed it before about her losing control." Becky started to turn away, stopped and added. "Last time was when Max went missing."

Max! Could it be?

Nik left Becky with a smile of thanks and headed to the

office where he could use the burner phone and call his brother. Something was wrong, he knew it. And... he had more proof when the phone didn't get answered. He called his mother's number and she picked up instantly. "Mom, what's Justin's phone number? I gather you have him tailing me, right?"

"Of course. From the minute I knew about you, he's been watching your back. Here's his number. Can I ask why you need him? And do you want any more like him? I can have a posse wherever you are in a very short time."

"No doubt. I'll let you know. For now, since he's close by, he'll do. I just need a ride and most of the squad's already left the office."

"Oh-kay! I won't ask why, but when you get a moment, we need to sit down and have a talk, share information."

"Good idea, we'll do it soon. Bye."

"Bye, son. Love you."

He hesitated too long and heard the click. The moment was lost. It had been the first time in his life that anyone had said that to him. It registered, big time.

Shaking off the pang of sadness, he called Justin. "Man, are you close by?"

"Yep. Need anything?"

"Wheels."

"Be there in a second. Meet me at the front door."

***

"When I asked for wheels, I meant without the driver." Nik glared at his companion behind the wheel.

"And my job is to follow you. How can I do that if I don't have a car?"

Shaking his head in disgust, Nik glowered at the smiling fool. "Just go."

"Where?"

"Maya took off and left me behind—"

"I saw her. She hit the road like a bat out of hell. Something had that woman stirred up."

"We got the warrant for the Smiths. But she didn't wait for me. Sent me to get Max's vest from his locker, and then they all left—her and the backup. No doubt, I could have gotten a car, but I don't know the procedure and I wasn't about to ask."

"Yeah, well, you knew I'd be close by."

"Haven't you always been, since Nellie found out about me? Drive."

Justin broke into the traffic and peeled around the corner, taking a road Nik hadn't been on before. "Nellie looks after her own. You don't know how lucky you are to have a mother like her. She's built up Harkins to where it's a prosperous company, has over three hundred employees and is a successful, multi-million dollar operation. And she's done it by picking the right people, treating them well and gaining a reputation for being one of the best security firms in the state."

"What about Max?"

"What about him? He's turned a blind eye to what's been right under his nose. Wants no part of it! And hasn't quite figured out that Nellie is the actual boss."

"And..."

"And she needs you. To step in and take over. Just sayin'... The work is getting too hard for her."

"What about you?"

"There's too much for one person. We've been sharing, but it's getting past us. She'd always hoped to carry on until Max saw the light, but he's too blind—doesn't want the burden. He couldn't handle that level of responsibility anyway. He struggles with the job he has. But I've looked into your background, Lieutenant Commander Baudin. You're exactly what we need."

"Quit stroking me, asshole. Drive past slowly. They won't make this car and I want an idea of what's going on before I plan any moves."

"See what I mean? You're perfect."

Wanting to change the subject, Nik continued. "One question. How come Max didn't recognize you when I told him about the pain-in-the-ass stalker I'd acquired?"

"That's easy. Number one, he knows me as Justin. And number two, three and four... you most likely described me a blond gay guy wearing goofy clothes and acting deranged. Of course he wouldn't recognize me. Now if you'd described this devilishly handsome, young executive who works in a top position for one of New Orleans's finest Security firms, he... ah, yeah, he still wouldn't have recognized me. Max just has no idea about Harkins or Nellie's influence. He's a good man, Nik, but most times, he sees what he wants. Now, you take after her. From the minute you showed up, she's been walking on air. You're just the man we need."

"Yeah, yeah, so you said. What the hell? Maya's vehicle is parked down from the surveillance van and it's empty. She must be with Higgins. Let's check."

Justin pulled a sneaky u-turn and parked behind the FBI issue that Maya drove. He and Nik stepped out of the car, palmed their weapons and moved toward the van, carefully checking every direction.

They found the back door open and Higgins slumped, the bloody hole in his head evidence of a vicious crime.

Justin said what Nik was thinking. "Dammit! If she saw this, which we both know she did, you'd think she'd have waited for back-up."

"The rest of the team are nowhere around. Shit! She's gone in. Alone."

"Yes, they are. Look down on the side street. They're out of sight, waiting for orders. Something's wrong."

They started toward the swat team who were milling together. Or at least Nik did. When he turned to introduce Justin, the guy was gone... again. *Damn, that man could fade.*

"Where's Agent Barnes?" He approached the team leader and waited anxiously for an answer. "Not sure, Max. We figure she's gone inside. Found Higgins dead in the van, shot in the back of the head. Sent a man to get eyes on the situation but he hasn't come back. What do you want us to do?"

Realizing he outranked them, Nik knew he had to make some decisions. During the years he'd commanded in the forces, taking the lead had come naturally. Now, with his heart racing, panic choking him and sweat breaking out everywhere, he sensed a pivotal moment had come. Was he finished?

He stalled. "Who has the actual warrant?"

"Agent Barnes."

Before he could deliberate on the orders he knew they waited for, a whistle broke the silence and he just reacted. "Let's go. You four, get around the back. You," he pointed at the oldest on the team. "Take that truck and park it across the driveway so they can't leave. You three, come with me."

Chapter 63

Maya knew she was being foolhardy. She should have waited for the team, but any chance of saving Nik's life couldn't be ignored. With her gun clutched tight, palms wet, using the sleeve of her lightweight blouse, she wiped the sweat from her brow and brushed away the tears from her eyes,

Inching forward, she crept past the dried bushes and worked her way to the window. Peeking inside only made it worse. Her heart felt like it was taking the same beating Nik was actually experiencing. Two men held him while Smith junior worked him over.

Pissed, madder than she'd ever been in her life, she broke cover and ran to the door. If she could distract them, hold them off for a few seconds so Nik could get to her, they had a slight chance to make it to safety. Her team was right behind her. They'd be here any minute.

Dammit! That was her man getting hammered in there. Even though he wasn't Max, Nik also seemed to be more of a partner than Max had ever been. And more importantly, he was her lover.

Carefully, she opened the door to the outer office and waited until the skinny bookkeeper noticed her and her weapon. With her finger against her lips, she motioned for him to go into the inner office and using him as a shield, gun held to his back, she ordered, "Slow and easy. We go in and get Foster. No one gets hurt. Understood?"

His bony Adam's apple, traveling the length of his neck at a pace that must have made breathing difficult, he croaked. "Yes. Please. Don't hurt me."

"No one gets hurt. Go."

He reached over and opened the door. As soon as they crossed the threshold, he pulled away leaving her standing alone. With her gun now held in both hands, unwavering, she pointed it directly at Smith senior. "Call off Junior, or I will gladly color the front of your shirt blood red."

Everyone in the room froze. The man lying in a pool of blood right under the window certainly obeyed her instructions and she now knew why she hadn't seen him earlier. The other three assholes in the room looked to see what their boss wanted.

"Well there, missy. Knew you'd be coming sooner or later. I suspect since you've entered the premises, you've brought legal documentation to do a search. I've been expecting you. In any case, I do want to report a crime. The man who's been shot broke into my office and attacked me. I have witnesses to this. My men will corroborate what happened." The sleazy sicko waved his arm around the room to draw her attention away from him.

Her peripheral vision worked well and she saw the stupids waggling their heads in agreement. But her eyes never left the man in charge, nor did her gun waver. "And you're beating up Agent Foster, why?"

"He's an agent? The man stole some files from me. I

wanted them back and he's refusing to co-operate. Just a misunderstanding."

Disgusted with his attitude, Maya couldn't take any more of the crap he was dishing out. "I want everyone to put their guns down on the floor and go lean against the far wall." She motioned with her chin in the direction she wanted them to go. "And, Junior, you should know you're next on my most-wanted list. Assaulting a federal agent is just too stupid for words. There's pay-back involved. If you know what I mean?"

When no one moved she cocked the hammer of her gun, smiled directly at the old bastard and waited.

"Move, boys, don't you see the lady's serious?"

The bookkeeper stepped out to do her bidding first, and the others hesitated. The two holding up Nik let him fall back on the chair and slowly put their guns down as ordered, then they joined the skinny shit at the wall.

"Partner, you okay?" Maya couldn't look his way to see if he was still conscious. She whistled loudly, another trick she'd learned from a dear old step-dad. Hoping to get some response, her heart dropped when he didn't answer. Rightfully so, she took it to mean he was too injured to speak. Dammit! She could have used his help about now. "Hey, pipsqueak, you have hearing problems. I'd really like to shoot your dear dad in the same place he shot my man in the van. Tit for tat, you know? Don't try me."

"I'd keep your hands away from that drawer, Papa Smith. It's just the cause I'd need to shoot you – self-defense. Move, Junior, *now*."

"Okay, Agent." Smith junior lowered his fists and stepped right in front of her, blocking his dad from her view. *Not good!*

Everything happened at once. The door flew open and

Nik... *Nik?*

bolted between her and Daddy Smith, whose gun suddenly made an appearance. The few seconds it took for the old prick to comprehend this move were enough for the man—who could only be Max—to sprint from the chair, push Nik out of the way and take the bullet meant for him.

Then all hell broke loose. Men were scrambling for their guns. Maya, recovering quickly, put a bullet in Smith before he could get off another shot. Nik wrestled away the weapon Junior had found on the floor and put him down easily with one punch to the jaw.

Seconds later, the team were everywhere and had control of the room and its inhabitants. Maya, head spinning, searched for Nik and found him crouched next to his brother who lay crumpled on the floor, blood pooling rapidly from the wound on his head.

Oh Max!

Chapter 64

Maya stumbled to where Nik was leaning over his brother. "Dammit, Nik. I thought he was you. I had to come in... God, is he alive?"

Nik swung around and called out orders. "We need a medic. Now! This man's still with us, but he's losing blood fast." Nik's hand covered the bullet hole, trying to stop the flow. "Get me something to hold against the wound."

One of the team members pulled out a package from his SWAT suit, unwrapped the pressure bandage and handed it over. "This will work, sir."

"Thanks." Nik held the white compress against Max's head, then looked over at Maya, agony written in big letters over his features. "Baby, see if the ambulance is here, okay? We need to get him to the hospital as soon as we can."

Before she could stand, medics rushed in with a stretcher and hurried over. Pushing Nik out of the way, the leader did a quick assessment and smiled. "He'll be fine, it's not deep; it just grazed him. But head wounds bleed like a bitch. I think the beating he took did more harm.

Can you stay with him for a minute while I check with the other ambulance? Be right back."

Nik moved in close to Max and bent over him. "How did they get you out of Linda's? Is she okay?"

"I took off myself. Decided to go to the apartment and find you, wanted to make the switch, just couldn't stand the thought of you getting hurt. They must have had someone watching the place. They picked me up, brought me here and the rest you know."

"Bro, you shouldn't have done that. I'm fine."

"Yeah, well know I'm back and you can get on with your life."

"Okay, it'll all work out. Just get better."

The attendant returned. "We'll get him to the hospital and they'll put in some stitches. He'll get to keep his good looks." The mischievous grin faded when he looked up and realized he was talking to a replica of his patient.

Grinning stupidly, happier than hell, Nik grabbed the EMT's hand and shook it, repeatedly. "Thank you. He's my brother—"

"Older brother..." Max's voice, feeble but distinguishable, cut him off.

"Who says?" Nik heard the happy note he couldn't hide. Didn't care. His brother would live.

"Mom says. Favor... you tell her about me. Be there to catch her..."

"Will do, bro. Just rest now."

Before Nik could decide how he'd get over to Nellie's, one of Maya's team reported to them. "Just got word. We found the container."

Chapter 65

"What the hell do you mean it was empty?" Nik and Maya had stepped out to the ambulance with Max when Maya's phone vibrated. Hoping to the get the news about the container they'd found and that the girls were all alive, this startling twist left her reeling. "Shit! Okay, Junior's here. We'll talk to him. Thanks, Becky."

"Did you hear?" Maya turned to Nik, her distress making him step closer as if he could protect her from the disappointment by his very presence. She loved that he tried to show support without banal phrases. Though unspoken, she knew he'd understood her disappointment.

Max called out from inside the ambulance. "I heard it too. Bummer!"

Getting the nod from the ambulance driver, Maya and Nik climbed in beside Max. Maybe the oxygen they'd hooked him up to had helped, or they'd given him some drugs, or he was just so glad not to have some asshole pounding on him that he seemed more alert. "Just so you know, they shot that guy in the office because he'd messed up. I didn't hear everything, it happened after they'd been working me over for a while and I kinda lost track, but they were pissed at some information he delivered."

"Did you recognize him?"

"No, never saw the guy before. Poor sap had been sent to give bad news to a prick who didn't like hearing it. I figured for sure I was next. But they needed those files. And I never did get them. Bob, my snitch, didn't show up that night at the restaurant."

Little did Max know, but the man had showed up and put his life on the line to try and help him. And he'd brought the files just as he'd promised. Nik didn't think Max needed to know about any of this right now. After he got discharged from the hospital would be soon enough. "Rest now, you've earned it. And thanks for taking the bullet meant for me." Nik rubbed Max's shoulder affectionately.

"Hey, it's what brothers do."

Maya leaned over Max and kissed his cheek. "I was never so glad to see Nik bursting into the room. It meant you were alive. I'm glad."

"Me too. This way I'll get more time to spend with my big brother."

"I'm the oldest?" It was news to Nik. He couldn't stop the delighted chuckle.

"Only by a few minutes, jackass."

"I guess that counts, little bro."

Getting the signal from the driver that they wanted to leave now, Maya and Nik climbed out.

The ambulance doors began to close when Nik called out, "We'll be right behind you."

The doors re-opened and the attendant stuck his head out and pointed his thumb behind him. "Max says to go find the girls. Then come see him with good news."

"Tell him—will do." Maya grinned at Nik and said, "Now that's the partner I was searching for."

"He's something else, isn't he?" The pride in Nik's voice resonated with sentiment.

Maya knew Nik really didn't "get" her Max, the occasional lazy procrastinator with a dual personality. Sometimes, like for this case, the man dug deep and was the best on the team. And on other occasions, he just danced to his own tune.

To give the devil his due, his mean streak, the one he'd introduced to her early in their partnership, hadn't been seen in some time. Though he hid it well, Maya was always conscious that it festered and might appear at the weirdest moments and for the craziest reasons. Could genetics play a part even when it was the absentee parent who had the violent tendencies? She would have to ponder that another time. But...she understood completely why Nellie didn't see him as the leader that Harkins Security needed...

Nik broke into her thoughts and brought her back to the noisy yard where the police vehicles and law personnel were milling around everywhere; people with jobs to do and records to keep.

"I don't get it. They must have gone and picked up the girls right under our noses. I thought that Bitters had all the terminals covered?"

"Not possible. We don't have that much manpower. But we did have the videos working except that, according to Becky, the one closest to where they stored the container was busted... again."

"Inside job."

"Yeah. I'm going to pull Junior aside. See if he'll help us. Maybe the sniveler will be inclined to get his sentenced lowered after he finds out his mandatory minimum is up to fifteen years. Worth a try."

"Why not question the bookkeeper? He seems less likely to take the rap for the Smiths."

"Junior's got more to lose in the end. Plus, I can work him easier. I'll try anything. If these assholes get to those poor girls, they'll be lost to us for good."

Maya and Nik went back inside the office where the agents were reading rights and handcuffing the prisoners. "Hal, can we talk to Mr. Smith for a few minutes?"

"Sure. The one over in the corner bawling?"

"He's still crying?"

"Yep. Hasn't stopped. Thought he was worried about his old man getting shot, but when the old fart starting yelling at him to keep his trap shut, he just cried harder." Hal shook his head, disgust coloring his features.

"We want Junior."

"Have at him, but you might want to haul his ass to the outer office so the others aren't watching him blubbering to the law."

"No problem."

Chapter 66

Seeing the good sense in Hal's suggestion, Maya pulled aside one of the officers and gave him instructions. "Go get Junior and when you bring him out, just mention loudly that his limousine has arrived or some such foolishness. Then bring him to the outer office. Make it look good."

"My pleasure, ma'am."

Having time alone, Maya walked up to Nik and leaned her head on his chest, her hands on his hips. And refrained from letting her body get too close or she'd be in his arms. Nik whispered, "Why didn't you wait for me?"

"Lassiter called. Said they had you. I went crazy."

"I couldn't find the locker room and when I came back, you'd left. I had to get Justin to drive me here."

"That man sure does come in handy. I'm glad."

They both heard the commotion at the same time and pulled back from each other. Nik whispered, "Tonight."

Maya's stomach flipped over and her pulse sped up. *Oh, yeah!*

A few minutes later, Maya, with Nik at her side, faced the criminal. "Sit down, Mr. Smith." Nik made sure he complied by forcibly lowering him into the chair Maya had set up in the corner.

"This is just an informal chat, between friends if you like."

"Since when did you become my friend?" Smith sneered then sniffed, his snotty nose a problem, as were the tears still pouring over his cheeks.

"Since you have information I need and I have a deal for you." Maya waved over the younger cop. "Officer, can you uncuff him please?"

Once freed, Smith wiped his nose on the short sleeve of his white shirt, the resounding snort turning Maya's stomach.

"I have nothing for you, bitch. You think I'll be a stool pigeon on my own gang?"

"Not your gang, your step-father's. The same man who called you a stupid kid who takes after his actual dad—a loser. The only reason he let you into the office was because your mom insisted. Guess she didn't want you around either."

Another wail broke loose and the kid started up again. Nik stepped in and laid his hand on Smith's shoulder. "Hey, son, don't take it so hard. I had a son-of-a-bitchin' dad too, only he was my own blood. The Bastard treated me like shit. It happens."

Maya stepped back and let the smooth-talker take over. *How cool was this?* Nik was almost singing the words in the velvet tones he'd used on stage to win her over.

Smith looked up at Nik, his eyes filled and his voice pitiful. "He's a real prick, makes me work all the time and never tells me nothing. Expects me to run the show when I'm always left in the dark."

"Predictable. Doesn't want to share control. Assholes

like him think we're blind and brainless. Do all the work and see nothing. Well, that's not the way things are, right?"

Junior sat higher in his chair, his shoulders against the back, his feet straight on the floor, listening, sucking in the bullshit. "I see and hear plenty."

"I just bet. For instance, does the stupid son-of-a-bitch let you look after the shipments he gets, you know the special ones?" Nik leaned closer, lowered his voice and winked.

"No. But he blames me when things go wrong. I thought he was going to shoot me earlier when Doug came to tell him that the girls had escaped. Wasn't my fault. Hell, they never even let me near the terminal. Just stayed in the office and manned the phones. What kind of crap is that? It doesn't take a man to answer the damn phones."

"Then I guess you filled the bill perfectly, sweetheart." Maya patted his cheek, just a bit harder than necessary. "Thanks for the info. Let's go, Nik.

"Hey, wait, what about the deal?"

"No need, dummy. You already gave us what we needed."

Nik followed Maya as she headed for the car.

"What's up?"

She turned. A huge smile lit her features. Grabbing his hand and squeezing, she began to laugh. Then she hugged him. "Come on."

Chapter 67

From the moment they got into the car, Maya leaned Nik's way and nestled into his arms. Nik, reeling from her apparent distress, just held her and repeated "Shush" over and over. No one had ever cared about him this much before and he didn't know quite what to do with all the emotion. Seriously upset, having suffered through seeing him being beaten—or who she thought was him—he gathered she was acting understandably needy.

"I'm fine, baby. Don't cry. It wasn't me in the chair." Nik soothed her, his hands caressing her hair and his kisses landing everywhere he could reach, which was as much of a balm to him as it was to her.

Sniffling, still clinging, Maya whispered. "I could have lost you."

"You didn't. And never will. I'm fine."

"I couldn't take it if something happened to you now. I'd want to die." Her words sent shivers racing over his body. She was deadly serious.

"No one's dying. I'm not in any danger."

"You will be if you re-enlist." The silence lasted as long

as it took his brain to understand her meaning.

"I won't go back. Don't think I'm operational any-way—too much psychological damage. I could head up a security company and stay in New Orleans though." Now where the hell had that come from?

The bevy of kisses she scattered all over his face, plus her delighted squeals, revealed he'd come up with the per-fect solution. One that also felt right to him. He could do just as he'd proposed and it would make him happy.

Working together, he'd get to know his mother and, as Justin had told him earlier, no doubt as a bribe, the job would be right up his alley.

Nik held her away and made her meet his eyes with her own shining green wonders. "But what about you, darlin'? How am I supposed to handle the fact that you're in dan-ger every day?"

"I'm not. Not really. Since you've been working with me, things have been abnormally crazy. Trust me; we don't put in weeks like this very often. There's seldom any real risk. And besides, I have Max to keep me safe."

He breathed easy. "That's true." Just knowing she'd be under his brother's protection lifted the weight off him immensely. Okay, why was she smiling like that?

"We need to move. I just had to hold you for a little while."

"Where're we going? I gathered from your earlier happy glow that you know who has the girls. And since Justin disappeared a while ago, I'm surmising it has some-thing to do with him."

"Of course! That's why they shot the man in the office, who's still alive, by the way."

"I know. I saw the medics working on him. They got a pulse. Can't believe even these creeps would cold-bloodedly shoot one of their own. Hope the poor bastard makes it to the hospital."

"Junior said the reason they'd turned on him was because of the bad news he'd brought, right? The girls were gone. So, the only other ones looking for them was your mom's firm, Harkins."

"So we're off to Nellie's house."

Laughing, Maya started the engine and pulled away from the curb. "Don't let her hear you say that."

Chapter 68

Melee traveled in a car with the blond man called Justin. He'd promised to drive Solada to the hospital, but who knew whether his word was good or not? She couldn't take the chance. Armed with the knowledge of what had befallen some of the other girls who'd disappeared from her area, Melee had decided to stay beside her friend.

She looked out of the window at the dark world and felt closed in and terrified. He could do with her as he wanted. No one knew where they were. The other men had scrambled the girls into a van and left so quickly, it made her head spin.

"Those men who took the others, where are they going?"

"Don't worry, sweetheart. They're safe now and will be looked after."

Since she was the only one who'd stuck with Solada, the only one who'd cared; she hugged her little friend closer and prayed.

The man spoke to her, his voice kind. "Do you know of a girl called Mai Cruz?"

Melee had never heard of her. What should she say? Scared to tell him no, she almost admitted to a friendship, but at the last moment, honesty stopped her. "No. I don't think so."

The man called Justin turned to her. "We're almost there. Keep trying to give her sips of water. Not too much."

Melee had questions. Should she ask? Would he stop the car, drag her from the back seat and beat her? She didn't think so. Taking a deep breath, she hesitated a few more moments and then began. "You said we were safe. But what will happen to us?"

"My boss, a nice lady called Nellie Foster, owns a huge security company. She'll make arrangements with a government agency and get all of you the visas you need to return home. And it'll happen quickly. Don't worry. There's nothing to be afraid of."

Melee believed him. Her heart raced with thankfulness and she accepted that his sincere words were true. "Thank you. I've been so scared."

"I'm sure you were...Melee, is it?"

"Yes."

"Well, young Melee, you have nothing to be afraid of from now on. You will be taken care of."

***

The black SUV that smashed into his trunk was as unexpected as the scream from the child sitting behind him. Stupid bastards obviously hadn't heard that the game was over. They were still after him. Shit!

He floored it at the same time as yelling at Melee. "Get down on the floor and pull your friend with you, small as you can get."

"What's happening?" Fear made her voice break.

"These fellows have a problem with me, honey, not

you. Don't worry. This car can outrun anything on the road." Proving his words to be true, Justin hit the gas and the phone switch on the steering wheel at the same time. When the voice asked him who he wanted to talk to, he gave it a number.

"Yo, Justin. What's up?" Nik sounded like he was in the car sitting beside him.

"Hey, sugar. I have a car on my tail trying to climb up my backend and need some help if you have any handy."

Maya's voice came on instantly. "Where are you?"

While he maneuvered the car around the corners on the highway they were traveling, Justin gave her the directions. Thankfully, there wasn't a lot of traffic because the jerks in the SUV behind were playing for keeps. They wanted him—preferably dead.

"Okay. We're close. I'll head over your way and meet up with you at the next junction. I'll put out an APB to see if there're others in the neighborhood who can help. Hang in there."

"Just cruising along, honey. But don't take too long. I have a sick girl with me who needs a doctor."

Chapter 69

Within seconds, Maya pulled her usual tricks, flying down an embankment, cutting through a highway lane going the wrong way and hitting the other side on two wheels.

"Jesus save me from crazy female drivers!"

"Max used to say the same thing."

"I said it out loud? Sorry."

The appreciative laughter in Maya's voice made him grin. "He used to say that too. We're pretty close to Juli...I mean, Justin; the intersection will be coming up in a few minutes. Can you hit that button there on the radio and say what I tell you?"

Finished with the call-in, Nik tried to relax and not watch the other cars that were looking like they were standing still. The siren got most of them moving to the right. But there were always a few stragglers, and Maya took care of these by angling onto the shoulder and speeding past.

Relaxed in her seat, she handled the wheel with a casual flair that had him feeling envy and pride entwined with his panic. Her hands didn't grip the wheel but slid along it as if it were a living thing and she was stroking it, loving it. The machine did her bidding and she, in turn, paid homage.

Heartbeats ramping up, he looked away. The full moon was high and glowing in the middle of the front window. It was pretty. *Just think about the damn moon and breathe before you pass out.*

"There he is, just making the turn."

Nik looked to where she was pointing and added. "Both hands on the wheel, please. I see him" He was proud that his voice didn't waver with the anxiety he'd been fighting.

She laughed and had the audacity to wink at him before she pulled a crazy stunt and hit the grass. They drove across the barrier and cut off the SUV forcing them into the ditch. Managing to control *her* vehicle, the driver of the other wasn't nearly as good behind the wheel as Maya. The SUV flipped twice before landing on its hood. The wheels spun, grass flew in every direction and the motor roared with disapproval for the treatment.

Slowing and turning off her siren, Maya returned Justin's honk before he sped away.

"Careful. Someone might be waiting for us." Before she got out of their vehicle, Maya drew her gun, waiting for Nik to do the same.

She circled around to the left of the upside-down mess while he automatically took to the right. Crouching, caution uppermost in his mind, he moved quickly, wanting to get there before Maya approached. He could barely make out two passengers, both hanging, seat bags deflated and falling in front of them. Not taking any chances, he approached with caution and waved her back. "Hold it. One of them is moving. Stay there."

He heard an oath as one of the passengers released his seat belt and dropped. The car rocked as the man tried to get his feet under him. All of a sudden, he heard an unmistakeable sound and dropped to the ground as the bullet whizzed past. Wishing he'd taken the same path as Maya, he called out, "Honey?"

"I'm fine."

Nik crab-crawled closer to the smash-up and roared, his voice harsh with command. "Stop that shooting, you idiot. We've got you covered and the cavalry is coming. Listen." Sirens could be heard in the distant screaming their warnings. "Just throw out your gun."

Another shot rang out, this time smashing through the windshield.

"Hey, Nik," Maya called out. "Can you smell the gas?"

Picking up on her thought wave, Nik smiled with pride and answered. "Yeah! Wouldn't want to be trapped in that car if it catches. If we return fire, as we have every right to do, the whole mess could blow up. Boom!"

"Boom! My thoughts exactly."

Suddenly, a gun flew through the broken window and landed in the grass about two feet from the car. "Okay, okay, I give up. Get me out of here."

Maya answered. "Is your partner alive?"

"Who cares, he's my driver. Just get me out."

Nik circled around quickly and came up behind Maya. He called softly, "It's me."

"I know. Or should I say my body knows. It's the craziest thing."

Nik pointed toward the screamer in the car. "He's a sweetheart, isn't he?"

"We'll leave him for the police to deal with. I just want to go to Nellie's and then go home with you."

"To sleep, right?"

"That too."

Chapter 70

By the time Nik and Maya got to Nellie's, she had all the girls organized, beds set up in various rooms and had just opened the door to her second-in-command.

"Justin, good, you all got here together. I've been going crazy. What's happened? How did you eventually find the girls?" She led the way into the kitchen and took cold beer and water from the fridge to place in in the center of the table so they could all choose what they preferred.

Maya gratefully reached for a beer at the same time as Nik. "Justin, you start." She was anxious to verify her assumptions as to the role he played in saving the hostages.

After he drank down a good half of his beer, he agreed. "Okay. First of all, I got a call from Paul with the container information Doug had passed on. We showed up there before the others and got the girls out quickly. We sent them here, all but Solada and Melee who, as you know, are now in the hospital."

"And..." Nellie drilled him.

"They're both fine. Solada has heat stroke, but she'll

recover. And that Melee... what a little trooper? She sure kept it together during the excitement. In fact, she worried about her little friend more than herself. In the end, she opted to stay with her at the hospital so I made the arrangements."

"There was trouble?" Shrewdly, Nellie picked up on his meaning.

"Nothing that couldn't be handled with the help of the Feds." He grinned at Maya and Nik. "I'll fill you in later, boss lady."

"Fine. What about the boys?"

"Okay, don't get upset, but the gang members made Doug go back with them to give the bad news to Smith. From what I understand, the crazy old prick shot him. But he's going to make it."

Maya had to ask. "Who are Doug and Paul?"

Justin answered, "Two of our operatives who'd infiltrated the gang a while ago. They were quasi-dock workers and paid off by the Mosleys to look the other way during certain consignments. This was the first time Doug was used in one of their special shipments. Damn shame he had to get shot. Guess the others knew what to expect from their crazy-ass boss and none wanted to be the bearer of bad news."

Nik added. "The EMT's had him in the ambulance, said his pulse had strengthened. It really looked like he'd make it."

Nellie turned to Nik. "Okay, your turn. What happened at the Smith's office?"

Dreading having to tell his mom about Max, Nik gently took her hand.

"I promise you he's fine now, but Max took a bullet for me..."

"Max..."
He caught her just in time.

Chapter 71

Lying in bed together after an incredible session of love-making, Nik cuddled Maya close. He stroked her arm, his fingers feathering her soft skin which smelled wonderful. Loving the perfumed soap she used, he sniffed her neck and then licked the baby-soft skin.

"You like that?" he teased.

"I like everything you do." Man, her voice was sexy when she was aroused.

He kissed her hard. "Even this?" He kissed her again.

As soon as he let her speak, she answered. "Oh, yeah!"

"How about this?" He stroked her pale breast, visible in the darkened room.

"Uh-huh! I love that. A lot."

He let his hands travel down her stomach, sneak under the cover and search out the moist area he'd recently just visited. He inserted a finger, gently, rubbing the favored spot with his others. "And this..."

Her moan of excitement ripped at his control. His breathing quickened as once again, his body hardened, readying itself for another dip into pure, unequivocal delight. Man, he couldn't' seem to get enough of her.

She obliged by undulating her hips and rapping her warm arms around his back. Surprising the hell out of him, she flipped over and changed positions. Now, she lay, draped over his body, chest to chest, stomach to stomach with his hardness nestled close to her sweet spot.

With a little maneuvering, she joined them and then sat up. Riding him gently, her probing kisses adding to his pleasure and her breathing quickening with his, she muttered.

"Your turn. You like this?"

"Oh, God! More." He moaned. "Please. Don't stop."

Chapter 72

The next day, Nik and Maya were called to Nellie's to celebrate the case and they both couldn't wait to share their news with the one person who they knew would be the happiest for them.

"Hi, Mom." Nik said the words and hated the trickle of apprehension that still existed from the scared little boy hidden deep inside the man.

Nellie opened the door wider and waved them in. As if she sensed his desperation, her loving gaze directed his way settled his fear. Hugs shared, she asked, "Want to sit out on the porch for a while? It's cool there at this time of the day."

"Sure." Nik and Maya sat on the swing and Nellie settled into her chair. "Where's Justin?"

"As far as I know, he's gone to the hospital to check on Solada. At least he said he would be at the hospital. The girls' paperwork is coming along fine and we should be able to send them back to their homes by the end of the week. In the meantime, we've got some of the crew taking them around to the tourist spots."

"That's great news, Nellie." Maya couldn't help reaching across to the older woman and rubbing her arm in gratitude. "It makes me happy to know those babies have such a wonderful champion."

"When people can, they should. That's the motto I live by. You two are looking pretty silly, beaming at me, a secret at the tip of your tongues and no one willing to say what it is. For heaven's sake, tell me before I burst."

Nik laughed. "You still looking for a manager to help at Harkins?"

"Nope." Nellie turned sly, her face serious. "Never was looking for a manager."

Nik swung his gaze to Maya, his eyebrow rose when he saw the smile lighting up her face. *What's she so happy about? His world had just blown up.*

"Nik," Nellie took his hand, "I want someone to replace me as *the* CEO. I'm offering you that position and I hope with all my heart that you'll make an old woman happy. It's time I started watching soaps and eating bonbons."

He waited until they both had their eyes on him and then he answered, "Nope." *Two could play the same game.* Nik watched their expressions topple and this time he wore the stupid grin.

"The only way I'd ever take on that position is if I was trained by the incredible woman herself who built up the company. There's plenty of time later for being a lazy old woman. Is it a deal?"

Laughing, relief obvious from both of the ladies, one nodded and the other beamed.

Before they could say anything more, a car pulled up with a squeal of tires and a blonde woman jumped out, fury engraved over her features.

Nik stood, the knots in his stomach forming hard and fast.

The intruder stomped up the short path, flew up the steps and smacked Nik hard, right across the face. Both Maya and Nellie surged to his side.

"You bastard! Think you can get me pregnant and then take off, leave me high and dry after I've taken care of you for over a month? Well, it ain't gonna happen, darlin', you hear me?" Her voice rose and tears cascaded.

Linda!

Everyone stood, stunned. No one uttered a sound.

"*Max!* Do you hear me?"

Nik reached out just in time.

Nellie dropped right into his arms.

Afterword

Thank you so much for reading *Special Agent Maximilian*.

I loved writing this story and I hope you enjoyed reading it. If so, I would ask you for a favor. Wherever you purchased this book, please take a few minutes and leave an honest review. Authors enjoy hearing that readers like their stories, and hopefully, others will read your words and choose to buy the because of your sentiments.

My website at **http://mimibarbour.com** now has all my books listed with links to the various publishers to make it easy for you to return to where you bought the book and to find my other work.

While you're there, I'd really appreciate it if you would sign up for my newsletter so I can keep in touch.

http://mimibarbour.com/contact.html#newsletter

I only send out newsletters approximately once a month and you have my word that your address will never be shared.

Hugs, Mimi

Special Agent Finnegan

Book #2 in the blockbuster series *Undercover FBI* by
New York Times Best-selling author Mimi Barbour.

Love for his father makes a man weak- what'll happen if he
gives his heart to a woman?

*When Special Agent Finnegan O'Reilly gets shot, and the
news brings on his father's heart attack, he decides to take leave
from further undercover assignments. The O'Reilly has suffered
enough and Finn can't be the cause of more distress for this
beloved old rascal. Then his boss forces one more case on him – to*

take place in their own pub. Acting as the target to expose serial, suicide killers rampaging through New York City, Finn must play the part of a wife-beater, a cheating husband and an all-time jerk. No problem, until he meets his make-believe wife.

Renée Knight enjoys her job as a New York City cop. Her disguises have become a permanent fixture in her life, and no one knows what she really looks like. Except for the father she loves fiercely... the man, whose suicide makes no sense. If it means going undercover in an Irish pub where the culprits hang out, she's their girl. Playing the wife of the bar owner to catch the killers—easy. But they never intend for her to fall for this guy, she does this all on her own. Now she has to hire the assassins to arrange his suicide. Can she catch them, before they complete the mission?

The Vegas Series

This sizzling box set for the Vegas Series starts off where we meet up with hardworking, hard-assed Detective Aurora Morelli. Attempting to arrest a rapist who attacks her colleague then continually thwarts her attempts to bring him to justice—to a horrific nightmare where her new baby is kidnapped—this scrappy detective does everything in her power to control these events. Kai Lawson, a partner she doesn't want, fights against and in the end accepts (in her job and in her bed) is the hero in these first few stories. The bald-headed, purse-carrying hotshot knows just how to pull her crank and the outcome is entertaining. Their blockbuster story will get you totally invested in this series.

In the last three books, along comes Lisa Jordan, a kick-ass kinda gal who loves wearing the shield as a Vegas detective and enjoys the more strenuous aspects of her job. She steps in for a while as Aurora's partner while Kai is MIA. Her story begins here and ends the series as she fights her attraction for wealthy casino owner, Jeff Waters. After one wild night, the charismatic charmer digs his way into her heart and that of the three-year-old nephew in her care. The fact that he leaves her speechless, literally, detracts from his appeal for Lisa since as a self-professed chatterbox, it's the first time ever. On the other hand, everything else about the man is fascinating. She can no more fight her memories than stop herself from rescuing him from two killers holding him hostage in revenge for the mistakes of his father.

Praise for the Vegas series:

"Cops & drama, absolutely loved this series!" ~ reviewed by luvbooks

"Good action and great stories. What a bargain!" ~ reviewed by Johnny Rotten Apples

"Great story lines, wonderful characters!" ~ reviewed by Rachel Larson

"Bloody fantastic!" ~ reviewed by Bernadette Boyce

A word about the author

Mimi Barbour lives on the beautiful East coast of Vancouver Island and fills her days with writing and promoting her work. The rest of her day is spent in her garden, doing minimal housework, and visiting with her husband while he cooks their dinner.

"The favorite part of my job is meeting the characters from each new book. Designing them the way I want and having them act however I think they should. It's thrilling, especially when most of my make-believe folks are so very interesting. They're fun and surprising, and in most cases, people I would love to interact with in reality."

Contact me:

My website: http://www.mimibarbour.com/

Or my blogspot: http://mimibarbour.blogspot.com

Or follow me on twitter: https://twitter.com/MimiBarbour

Or on Facebook: Mimi Barbour Fan page

Please sign up for my fun Newsletter:
http://mimibarbour.com/contact.html#newsletter